SHARPS AND SPRINGFIELD
EQUALIZER

MORGAN BRICE

Equalizer

Sharps & Springfield
Book 2

Morgan Brice

eBook ISBN: 978-1-64795-088-0
Print ISBN: 978-1-64795-089-7
Equalizer, Copyright © 2025 by Gail Z. Martin.
Cover by Deranged Doctor Designs.

Darkwind Press is an imprint of DreamSpinner Communications, LLC

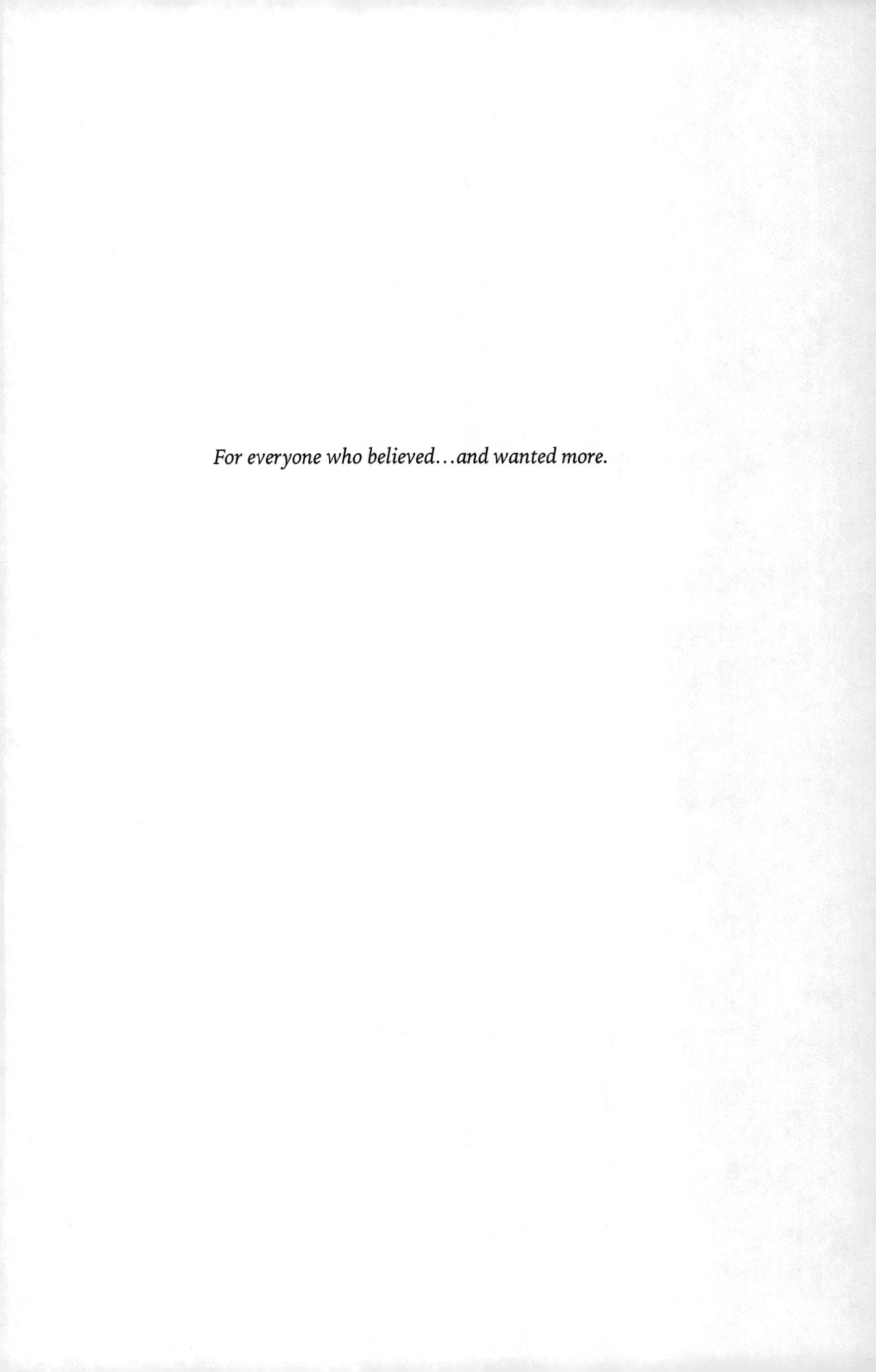

For everyone who believed…and wanted more.

Chapter 1
Calvin

Grave robberies? Doesn't it seem strange to send two federal agents to look for missing bodies?" Owen Sharps reached for a slice of warm bread. The rocking of their Pullman car gently sloshed the tea in his cup.

"Seems they think there's more going on than medical students getting cadavers to study." Calvin Springfield added a liberal smear of peach jam to the butter on his toast and paused to take a gulp of some coffee.

"Plenty of creatures steal corpses, but they usually dig up the coffins after burial. They don't snatch bodies out of morgues without a trace." Calvin savored another sip of coffee, hoping it chased away the last vestiges of a poor night's sleep. "Headquarters must have had an inkling that this was our sort of problem."

Owen gave him a look. "Or they're still annoyed with us for breaking the rules on the last case."

Calvin sighed. "Or that. Although it was all for a good cause, and we did end up being right, after all."

"I guess if they wanted to give us a slap on the wrist, they'd send us to some god-forsaken cattle town in the middle of Wyoming instead of Chicago," Owen replied.

"Although Chicago is probably the biggest cattle town in the country," Calvin observed.

Winston, their butler, assistant, and bodyguard, appeared right on time to refill their cups and remove the plates. "I've checked the wire several times—no new telegrams, although that might change once we're in Chicago. I have to admit, I'm intrigued," Winston said.

The Pullman's gentle rocking contrasted with its speed as it hurtled down the tracks toward Chicago. The luxury private coach served as their cover as traveling businessmen and investors, hiding Calvin and Owen's work as agents for the Supernatural Secret Service. Although he took on the role of butler, Winston Smith was a highly-trained operative with experience in research and a dead-eye shot.

The Nighthawk-series sleeper car cut a handsome profile, gleaming black with chrome accents. Its generous observation platform opened into a well-appointed parlor with dark wood walls, a hammered tin ceiling, and furnishings in emerald green velvet, as befitted two wealthy gentleman investors.

Inside, the car featured a parlor with velvet-tufted couches and armchairs, side tables, and a large poker table. Three sleeping cabins each had a full-sized bed with a chair, desk, and private bath. A library with a telegraph station and floor-to-ceiling bookshelves provided opportunities for research as well as relaxation, and a hidden corkboard helped them organize information. A well-equipped lab accommodated medical, scientific, and arcane needs.

Large windows provided plenty of light in the dining room, with a mahogany table, dark green velvet draperies, matching upholstery, and glass-fronted cabinets filled with bottles of liquor and wine.

Winston presided over the kitchen and pantry, a well-qualified butler and bodyguard. Hidden shelves scattered throughout the car concealed racks of guns, knives, and other weapons.

Like its owners, the private car was more than it appeared, with steel walls and ceiling reinforced to stop most gunfire, and the window glass was an experimental prototype that would fracture but not shatter from bullets. A special air filtration system protected them from a gas attack, and the undercarriage could survive driving over a significant TNT explosion.

Given that their work dealt with the supernatural, every room except the laboratory had pipes of salted holy water with iron filings built into the window and door frames. Warding sigils against demons, dark magic, and an exhaustive list of supernatural nasties were worked into the steel behind the wood paneling.

The train lurched, nearly sending their cups into their laps. All three men grabbed for a handhold to keep from being thrown from their seats, and the train's brakes screeched.

"What the hell is going on?" Calvin shouted above the din.

"Don't know, but it looks like we're making an unexpected stop," Owen said.

Calvin went to the window. "I can't see anything from here."

"Must be serious—this is the express. It doesn't do extra stops," Owen said.

When the train finally stilled, Winston looked out the door. "I'll be back in a moment," he told them and hopped down to the siding. Through the window, Calvin saw Winston talking to three men in railroad uniforms who pointed in the direction of the engine.

Finally, Winston returned to where they waited. "We hit an automobile that was straddling the tracks. They're clearing the wreck. Made a mess of things. They think the driver was thrown clear—there's no body in the car."

Owen's eyes took on a distant glaze, and Calvin knew his partner was tuning in with his abilities as a medium to search for the spirit of the dead driver.

"He was gone before the accident," Owen said in a far-away voice as he listened to the voices from the other side. "Dead when someone put his car on the tracks."

"Does he know who killed him or why?" In the brief time he and Owen worked together, Calvin had gotten more comfortable with his partner's ability. Now Calvin thought of the ghosts as just another type of witness, although their appearance still sometimes gave him a fright.

Owen stared into the distance at things only he could see. "He didn't see his killer. He's very confused about why anyone would want him dead."

"That's an elaborate setup for someone without a motive," Calvin pointed out. "Can you get a name? Does he know where the killer left his body? We can follow up with the morgue once the police are through."

"Arthur," Owen said. "Arthur Simpson. He's still quite unsettled. It takes the newly dead a while to collect themselves. Dying is traumatic."

"There's a surprise," Calvin muttered. "Anything else?"

Owen shook his head. "He thinks his body is in the woods. Maybe he can tell us more later, but he's lucky to know that much."

Winston was ready with a fresh cup of hot tea laced with plenty of sugar to help Owen gather his wits and replace the energy of reading a spirit. Calvin sat with him, noticing the way Owen's hand shook and how he had paled with the exertion of communicating with the dead.

"Thank you. I know it costs a lot to do that." Calvin placed a hand on Owen's thigh in support.

Owen closed his eyes and sighed as he sipped the fragrant tea. "Every effort has a cost. Mine is just a little weirder than most."

"The railroad people will need time to clear the tracks before the train can move on, and then we still need to have the car put on a siding once we arrive," Winston pointed out. "We won't get settled until after everything is closed. You have time to rest before there's any chance of going to the morgue."

"Let's get some fresh air and have a look," Calvin suggested.

Calvin and Owen walked a short distance up the tracks, watching steam tractors haul away the wreckage as railroaders examined the tracks for damage. Night was falling, and the workers used torches to light the cleanup effort.

Trees lined the path of the tracks, set back from the easement. Calvin saw movement near the shadows and squinted for a better look, then caught his breath, eyes going wide.

The translucent figure of a headless woman in a gray dress stood at the edge of the shadows.

I'm not the one who usually sees ghosts. I've got to be imagining things.

"Owen? I need you." Calvin's voice sounded higher than usual, even to his own ears.

"I hope so," Owen replied cheekily, coming up behind him, then quickly sobering. "What's wrong."

"I saw a ghost. A headless woman. Out there." Calvin pointed toward the dark fringe of the forest, but the apparition was gone.

"There's no one now." Owen moved to stand next to Calvin.

"I don't think I just imagined it," Calvin said, still shaken. "Did I?"

Owen frowned. "People see ghosts all the time, regular folks who aren't mediums. Certain ghosts have enough energy to make themselves visible while others need someone with the right power to see and hear them."

"How are you so calm about this stuff?" Calvin stared into the darkness as if he could will the ghost to reappear.

Owen shrugged. "I've always had the Sight, and so did my mother and grandmother. Runs in the blood. The Church might not have liked it, but the neighbors believed."

"Why do you think she showed up?"

Owen led him back inside. Calvin sat, and Owen moved behind him to massage his tight shoulders.

"She probably haunts this stretch of rail from a long-ago accident and it's just a coincidence about her showing up now," Owen replied. "Or maybe the energy of the wreck drew her. When we get to Chicago, Winston can dig into the local lore. I'm sure there's a story to go with the haunting that's partly true."

"Do you think she caused the wreck?" Calvin tried to relax under Owen's firm touch, just realizing how tight his shoulders were from stress.

"Maybe. Depends on whether she has a reputation for harming people or whether she's just a harbinger. My bet is on the second choice. A lot of ghosts show up to warn the living about impending danger."

"She's a little late for the driver of the car."

"Maybe he wasn't who she was warning," Owen pointed out. "You're the one who saw her."

"You think we're in danger?" Calvin leaned into Owen's hands, trying to ignore how the connection affected him.

Owen chuckled. "We're government agents. We're always in danger. The question is—is it a supernatural threat or one from regular people?"

"Usually both," Calvin said with a sigh. "That's how it goes."

Owen shifted his hands to stroke the cords of Calvin's neck, then moved to rub at the tight muscles of his clenched jaw.

"Breathe." Owen bent to press a kiss to Calvin's hair. "Relax your jaw. You could crack a tooth."

"I don't know why this job has me jumpy," Calvin confessed. "It just feels like there's too much we don't know."

"Which is why we won't do anything without more information," Owen reassured. "While we're at the morgue, we'll see what we can find out about the accident. And I'm sure Winston will get all the details about the ghost from the workers at the station. We can reach out to Ida and see if any of her contacts might have details."

"Ida Tarbell knows everyone," Calvin agreed. The feisty journalist had made a name for herself with fearless reporting about corruption in high places. Her deep web of connections had proved helpful with another case, and Ida loved sussing out a good mystery whether she could publish the story or not.

"Seems like all the good journalists are named Ida," Owen said, remembering their friend Ida Hardin who had helped them out in St. Louis.

Winston returned with a triumphant smile. "I had several fascinating conversations with the chaps at the station. Let me get the roast in the oven, and I will share the details. In the meantime, why don't you gents relax with some port. We've still got a while until it's time to eat."

Calvin and Owen murmured their thanks. They closed the curtains in the sitting room for privacy and turned up the lamps.

"At this rate, we're not getting into Chicago until morning," Calvin groused, taking a seat on the sofa.

Owen sat next to him, a bit too close for propriety's sake. Their thighs touched and shoulders bumped. "Don't be in such a hurry. There will be plenty of time for us to chase down awful stuff once we get there. It's nice to get a bit of a breather before we go headlong into another bloody mess."

"You're right. I feel…twitchy," Calvin admitted.

Owen stretched up and brushed a kiss over Calvin's lips. "I can take care of that…after dinner."

"I was hoping you'd say that." Calvin grinned.

Their partnership and romance were still new, starting when they were assigned to work together and headed to St. Louis to tackle their first case. That success ensured that their pairing as agents was made permanent, along with using the Pullman car and Winston's services.

Falling in love hadn't been in the plan.

Their chemistry sparked from their very first meeting. Calvin had already been in the Supernatural Secret Service for three years, having served in the War Department before that. Back in Boston, Calvin honed his fighting skills with street gangs. His father, fearing that Calvin would end up dead or in prison, gave him an ultimatum: to enlist or be turned over to the police.

Calvin knew how to use charm and wit to make friends quickly and warm up reluctant contacts. At six feet tall with a trim, athletic build, Calvin stood out in a crowd even without his raven black hair, plush lips, and bright blue eyes with long, dark lashes.

Owen stood two inches taller with a rangy swimmer's build. His blond hair, fair skin, and green eyes were a striking contrast to Calvin's darker good looks. Owen's grandfather had opposed the Civil War and fled the South for Baltimore. A stint with the Army in the County Seat Wars and the Cattle Wars had been good preparation for Owen joining the SSS.

Chance threw Calvin and Owen together, and the spark between them burned brightly from their very first meeting. They learned to trust each other under fire and deepened that bond beneath the covers.

Calvin's stomach growled. "That roast smells good. I'm starving." He poured a glass of port for himself and one for Owen, and then they settled on the sofa as the car lurched to a start. Muted grumbling from the direction of the kitchen told Calvin that the jerky start had vexed Winston.

"Looks like they got the rails cleared."

"Let's hope the rest of the way to Chicago is less exciting," Owen remarked.

Calvin picked up his book from the side table and glanced toward Owen. "Didn't you just finish something?"

Owen nodded. "*The Time Machine* by H.G. Wells. That man has quite an imagination." He frowned, trying to glimpse the title of Calvin's book. "Did you start something new?"

Calvin chuckled. "I usually have two or three books going, depending on the mood. I started this one a week or so ago. *The Adventures of Sherlock Holmes* by Doyle—a British guy. Solid mystery, even if there isn't anything supernatural about how he solves the crimes. Brilliant, but a bit insufferable."

"I liked that book, but you're right—Holmes would be irritating as hell in real life."

"Hats off to anyone who solves crimes the hard way—without magic or being able to talk to the spirits," Calvin added. "Of course, Holmes has the benefit of being a work of fiction with an author who figures everything out behind the scenes. Must be nice."

Calvin felt the port warm him and loosen his tight shoulders. Despite Owen's excellent massage, Calvin still felt tense and feared that it was a harbinger of things to come. Much as he liked his book, he struggled to stay focused. His thoughts flickered back to the railway accident and his sighting of the headless ghost.

Could there be any connection to the new case? Seems like a stretch. Then again, things aren't always as random as they seem.

Winston summoned them for dinner, and Calvin startled at the interruption, having gotten thoroughly lost in his thoughts. He and

Owen joined Winston in the dining room, where a roast with boiled potatoes and carrots waited in the center of the table.

"That looks as good as it smells," Owen told Winston, and Calvin agreed.

"We need to keep you both in fighting form, and a good dinner goes a long way toward that," Winston replied, clearly pleased at the praise.

By agreement, they rarely talked about cases over meals unless the situation was dire. Winston made sure to pick up at least one newspaper at one of their stops throughout the day, and they competed to find the most interesting or unique tidbit to fuel their discussion.

Much of the news centered on the war with Spain or England's battles in the Sudan. It became a challenge to find stories that weren't related to either event to keep the conversation lively.

"It'll be interesting to see what that new Antarctic expedition discovers," Owen said. "Though I doubt we'll hear anything for quite some time. I can't imagine being at the very bottom of the world."

"No thanks," Calvin said. "What we do is risky enough. I have no desire to go somewhere entirely uncharted and freeze to death doing it."

"Chicago in late Fall isn't exactly toasty," Owen pointed out.

Calvin gave him a look. "It's not Antarctica."

"Admit it—you're curious," Owen teased.

"Curious enough to read an article or visit a traveling exhibition when—if—they get back? Yes. But I see enough strange things every day in this job without going to the ends of the earth." Calvin suppressed a shiver at the thought.

Winston refilled their drinks and served an apple pie for dessert. Calvin savored the smell of fruit and cinnamon mingled with the scent of fresh coffee. "You spoil us, Winston."

"Nonsense. Hard work deserves good food," Winston replied, although a smile tugged at the corners of his mouth.

Calvin had worried that Winston might reveal his and Owen's relationship to the authorities, which would get them fired and most likely jailed. To his relief, Winston supported them and kept their secret.

Winston was in his forties, about fifteen years older than Calvin and Owen, and a powerful witch and a skilled field medic, as well as a semi-retired field agent, chemist, and jack-of-all-trades. He played the part of their butler willingly, a ready cover for his presence. Winston stood a few inches short of six feet with a stocky build. His round face and spectacles gave him a bookish look, and gray tinged his beard and thinning brown hair.

Together the three men had proven to be comfortable traveling companions, taking on whatever unusual paranormal cases the SSS assigned them. After proving their mettle by thwarting vampires and stopping an attempt to open the gates of Hell, they had gained commendations and the notice of the top brass.

"In much less exciting news, there's a new cola," Calvin said, going back to their discussion of the news. "The inventor is calling it 'Pepsi-Cola.' Odd name, but I'd still try it if we happen upon a bottle. It's got me curious."

"You like all the soda fountain drinks," Owen teased. "You're like a kid with a sweet tooth."

Calvin shrugged. "Something different to try that isn't alcohol. It's a nice change, but I don't know that they'll ever really catch on."

"There's a galvanism exhibition at the big university," Winston remarked after a pause, keeping the conversation going. "I'm not sure how I feel about that type of thing, making severed hands and dead frogs twitch with electricity."

"Pretty creepy," Owen agreed. "But maybe something good will come of it. I'm not a fan of cutting up corpses, but doctors have learned a lot by doing it."

"You two have a strange idea of suitable dinner conversation," Calvin noted.

"We're hardly polite company," Owen smirked.

Winston shooed them out of the dining room once everyone was done eating, and they returned to the parlor for a nightcap of brandy. The train kept a steady speed to make up for lost time, and Calvin suspected their arrival wouldn't be delayed much despite the circumstances.

Calvin and Owen returned to their books, sitting close in easy silence as the brandy put the finish to a fine meal.

"I'll be in my room if you need me," Winston popped in to tell them. "If not, have a good night, and I'll see you in the morning."

"Thank you, Winston," Calvin replied.

"Goodnight," Owen added. Minutes later they heard the snick of the door to Winston's room. Owen tossed back the rest of his brandy and leaned toward Calvin.

"Ready to turn in?" He pressed a kiss to Calvin's neck.

Calvin turned toward him, guiding Owen's head with hands on either side until they were kissing on the lips. The kiss started light but quickly deepened.

They maintained separate rooms for deniability's sake since they dared not admit the truth to any but a few trusted allies. Most of the time, Owen slept in Calvin's room. While Winston willingly kept their secret, both men made sure to conduct themselves carefully in public. It helped that their roles as government agents kept them at a distance from most people and shrouded their lives in secrecy.

"Love you." Calvin's fingers traced Owen's sharp cheekbones and then the curve of his lips.

"Love you right back." The lightness of Owen's tone didn't hide the deep feeling in his blue eyes.

Tomorrow, they would be in Chicago and would need to take precautions to keep their secret, minding their tone and body language so that no one would suspect. Calvin knew that they needed to stay on the right side of the law and, more importantly, not give their supernatural enemies a weapon to use against them.

But right now, in the privacy of their rail car, hurtling down the tracks in the darkness protected by weapons and wardings, Calvin planned to wrap himself in the arms of his lover and pray for protection and deliverance to a god he wasn't sure was listening.

Chapter 2
Owen

No one saw the bodies being moved?" Owen focused his attention on the coroner while Calvin looked around the Cook County Morgue. Calvin bumped a corner of the desk and knocked a fountain pen on the floor, which he picked up and replaced in its spot after a momentary hesitation only Owen was likely to notice.

"I would have told the police if they had," Dr. Parker said sharply. He was a thin man with a prominent nose and pointed jaw, adding up to a hawkish appearance. "I'm probably more concerned than anyone over the sanctity of the bodies we handle here. But if you're thinking someone's pulling another 'Burke and Hare,' I believe you're wrong."

The two London body snatchers had their heyday seventy years before, but they remained infamous, synonymous with their crime and a boogeymen tale to frighten children.

"Why?" Calvin came back to stand beside Owen. They traded a wordless glance that Owen took to mean Calvin had seen something interesting but didn't want to comment in front of Parker.

"I'm still tied into the academic medical circles," Parker said. "If someone was supplying illicit dissection bodies, I'm pretty sure I would have heard. And after that big scandal forty years ago that the

Pinkertons cleaned up, no one legitimate would dare deal with body snatchers."

Owen had heard of that case. The police and the city government at the time were so corrupt that the city sexton himself had been found complicit in the crime.

"People will do just about anything if the money is good enough," Calvin remarked. "They always think they won't be the ones that get caught."

"I don't have any leads on the recent disappearances," Parker said. "But I did recognize the name of the guy they said had gone missing after the gas line explosion. Marvin Cobb, a reporter. He had been doing a story on the bodies that went missing."

Owen raised an eyebrow. "Interesting coincidence."

"Did you ever meet Mr. Cobb?" Calvin asked.

"More than once. The guy was relentless, which I guess is good in his line of work, but I'm betting he went poking the wrong people," Parker replied. "Polite enough, but he was like a dog with a bone. I didn't have anything to hide, but I got tired of him showing up with questions after every incident. If I knew anything—and I didn't—I'd have already told the cops, not a reporter."

"Do you have any idea of who else Cobb might have spoken with?" Owen believed Parker but couldn't shake the hunch that they were missing something.

"There's the city morgue and ours," Parker answered. "We're the big ones. But every local hospital has to have a place to keep the dead until the bodies can be sent on, even if they aren't equipped to do autopsies. The same is true for the big institutions like sanitariums, orphanages, and the mental asylum. People die, and either families claim them, or they're sent to the potter's field."

"You think Cobb made the rounds?" Owen asked.

"He seemed like a thorough guy, so I figured he would. I don't know all the people who run the other morgues—we don't have a secret coroner club—but I've met some of those men, and they don't seem the type to make an easy buck off the dead," Parker said.

Owen withdrew a card from his wallet and handed it to Parker.

"We'll be in town for a while, so if you hear anything you think we ought to know, you can contact us here."

Parker took the card and frowned. "Why is the Secret Service so interested in missing bodies? No one famous or important has been taken."

"National security," Owen fibbed. "Until we know what the body thief is doing with the corpses, we don't know the extent of the criminal activities involved. Best to nip the problem in the bud."

The coroner pocketed the card. "I doubt I'll come across any new scuttlebutt, but I'll let you know if I do. This sort of thing is bad for everyone. Erodes confidence in the system. Bereaved families shouldn't need to worry about such things."

They thanked Parker and headed back to their rented carriage. Despite being a cold, gray day, the sun made Owen squint after the cellar morgue.

"You think he's telling the truth?" Calvin asked.

"Yeah, I do. There's clearly something organized going on, but I don't think Parker is part of it," Owen replied. "Did you read anything from his pen?"

Calvin wasn't a medium like Owen; his ability was psychometry, the ability to read the history of objects by touching them. "He's generally grumpy, thinks he's overworked, and resents his boss," Calvin replied. "I didn't pick up any of the nervousness I'd expect if he were involved in something illegal. I don't think he's a risk-taking kind of guy."

"I guess there are worse things to touch in a morgue than a pen," Owen remarked.

Calvin rolled his eyes. "Much worse."

Owen and Calvin entered the carriage, where Winston waited as their driver. He had a city map spread out on the driver's seat next to him.

"Where to next?" He gave the horses a gentle tap of the reins.

Owen thought for a moment. "If the body snatchers can spirit corpses out of the largest morgue in the city, what have they been doing with the smaller ones that are probably less well-organized?"

"It begs the question of how many bodies they need and what they're doing with them," Calvin pointed out.

"There aren't a whole lot of options," Owen replied. "Either we've got a crazy necromancer raising an army of the dead—which I think someone would have already noticed—or they're being used for some sort of experimentation."

"So many?" Calvin asked. "We've heard of ten so far."

Owen shrugged. "Bodies don't keep, even if someone puts them in a refrigerator. And unless the thieves have taken to doing murder, people might not die at convenient times when a new corpse is needed. Which would explain the grave robberies."

In addition to bodies disappearing from the City Morgue, Calvin and Owen had caught whispers of recent incidents at the paupers' cemetery, where the thieves might have figured no one cared enough to investigate.

"Let's check out the institutions and then the smaller hospitals," Calvin suggested. "They probably don't have the same level of security." He gave Winston the name of the next place to visit.

Owen also suspected that the residents of the asylum and sanitariums might not have any family to notice their deaths or the means to raise a fuss if they did.

"I'm curious to see what use the bodies are being put to since the robbers don't seem to be picky about the cause of death," Calvin said as they jostled along. "For a medical school, they could make a lesson out of whatever the poor bastard died from. But usually people want their raw materials in good shape."

"Raw materials? God, Calvin."

"Think about it," Calvin persisted. "Maybe it's a crazed chemist trying to distill the elixir of life out of brains and livers or some such. I've heard theories that someday doctors could take an organ from one body and put it into another and have the receiving person improve."

"From a dead body?" Owen echoed, horrified.

"Some fellow took part of a thyroid from one person and stitched it into someone else, and the guy who received it lived—and did better," Calvin replied. "That was more than ten years ago. The research raises all kinds of uproar from the Church and plenty of ethics worries, but it's clearly possible."

"Damn. So what do you think? Rich people finding a match and stealing parts from poor blighters?"

Calvin shrugged. "Could be. Wouldn't be out of character. They steal everything else."

Owen frowned, thinking. "If there's money involved, the Mob is usually quick to find an angle. Do you think they're tangled up in this? Think about it—some desperate rich guy hires a mobster to find a match for whatever he needs, and the Mob delivers. Mobsters do worse than rob graves on a daily basis."

"That's an angle I hadn't considered," Calvin said. "But you're right—the Mafia doesn't usually miss a trick if there's a business opportunity. If that's true, then we need to watch our backs. They won't like us butting in on their venture."

They headed for Dunning Asylum. "Hold up," Owen said sharply. Winston paused as the massive, rambling structure came into view.

Calvin gave Owen a worried look. "What's wrong?"

Owen winced at the press of spirits around him, reaching out with empty eyes and grasping hands, warning them away and clutching at their warmth.

"So...many...ghosts," he managed.

Calvin pressed a small bag of salt into Owen's hands, and the ghosts receded, giving him a chance to catch his breath. "They're warning us away," he said a few minutes later. "Telling us that if we come here, we'll never be allowed to leave. They weren't."

Everyone in Chicago had heard of Dunning Asylum. It had grown from a poorhouse to include a tuberculosis sanitarium, a hospital for the mentally ill, and a large cemetery where unclaimed bodies from the general public were sent for burial, as well as the asylum's dead residents. Conditions were rumored to be abysmal, and adults often threatened children that they would be sent to Dunning if they misbehaved.

"That's certainly cheery," Calvin said. "Your call—go on or go back? The press of souls is likely to get worse." He reached over and took Owen's hand, hidden beneath their heavy cloaks.

Owen appreciated Calvin's concern and took a moment to sort his impressions. The ghosts frantically cautioned them but made no move to cause harm.

"We need to talk to the asylum's coroner," Owen said. "This would be an ideal place for bodies to be stolen. People end up here because they have no one to look after them. No one would be asking for their remains to make arrangements when they die, either."

The massive Kirkbride-style hospital stretched across the ridge of the next hill, with Richardson Romanesque towers and turrets like a dark mage's castle.

"The original idea for the design was noble," Owen mused aloud. "Trying to maximize light and air to the rooms and hallways instead of a big box. The hospitals were considered enlightened and revolutionary—but according to the reformers, the reality hasn't lived up to the ideals."

Winston drove them up to the front entrance. "I'll be over there." He pointed to an area for coaches. "In case we need to make a quick exit." He patted the broad sweep of his cape to indicate his gun.

"Hoping that's not needed," Calvin said under his breath. Owen had a strong suspicion otherwise.

They were dressed in suits and cloaks, so their appearance gave no pretext to turn them away, and they walked in through the main doors as if they belonged. Signs directed them to the morgue, although even without them, Owen would have guessed the basement.

His mental shielding kept the ghosts at bay, although it didn't mute them completely. Those who didn't try to speak to him flitted past them in the hallways, still trapped even after death. Most of those pale revenants were repeaters, wispy images that no longer retained much of the spirit's personality or memory.

Newer, stronger ghosts watched them pass with baleful glances and flashes of erratic energy. Thanks to the salt and silver they carried, as well as protective charms and the matching warding tattoos Owen had recently talked Calvin into getting, the ghosts didn't try to harm them, but Owen couldn't imagine how the hospital workers faced spending their days within the haunted halls.

"This is a huge building," Calvin murmured. "Like a castle of the damned." Owen noticed that Calvin kept his right hand clasped on his left wrist, doing his best to avoid touching anything.

The ghosts are bad enough. I wouldn't want to know what the walls remember.

"Good intentions gone horribly wrong," Owen replied. They found the morgue, and Owen opened the door.

The smell of formaldehyde and decay assaulted them when they stepped inside. This morgue was easily as large or larger than the one at the county hospital, reminding Owen of how many people were sent here and never left except in death.

At the moment, no one was in sight. Calvin and Owen seized the opportunity to have a look around, taking in the number of slabs and drawers and the general condition of the space. It wasn't quite as tidy or organized as the County Hospital, making Owen wonder whether that spoke to the professionalism of the staff or the burden of a constant influx of the dead.

"What are you doing here?" A florid-faced man with thinning gray hair bustled in from the next room. He wore a white lab coat, and his expression of righteous indignation suggested to Owen that they had just met Dunning's coroner.

"We're investigating the recent disappearances of bodies from morgues, and we'd like to ask you a few questions." Owen left out sharing their credentials for the moment.

"I don't know anything about that. You're not authorized. Get out," the coroner snapped. "You can't just barge in here."

"This is public property," Calvin pointed out. "And the public has a right to know if their family members' remains are being treated with respect."

The coroner gave a bitter laugh. "You think they care? Those families didn't give a damn about these poor bastards when they were alive. They'd probably thank someone for Burking the body and saving them burial expenses."

Owen hadn't expected quite such a cold assessment, even if he suspected it might be true for many of the patients.

"Do you think that's what happened?" Calvin picked up on the coroner's slang term for body snatching. "Families offering the dead to someone who will take the corpse off their hands?"

"That's not what I said," the doctor protested, going pale. "You're twisting my words."

"We asked about missing bodies. You brought up body thieves. We're just looking for answers," Owen replied levelly. The doctor's agitation made him wonder whether the man just took umbrage to having his reputation tainted or had darker reasons for fearing investigation.

"I don't have anything to tell you," the doctor maintained as his initial discomfort morphed into rage. "Get out, or I'll have security throw you out."

Calvin and Owen exchanged a look. "Sounds like you're covering something up." Owen hoped to provoke the coroner into revealing something useful.

"There are over one thousand patients here, nearly all of them in a bad way. Tuberculosis, scurvy, mental problems, all the things that come with too much alcohol and too little good food. They have one foot in the grave when they're sent here. We do the best we can. The last thing we need is a couple of muckraking reporters stirring up trouble. Get out."

Calvin and Owen exchanged a look, and Owen gave the man an inscrutable smile. "Suit yourself."

"What does that mean?" As angry as the coroner was, Owen saw a hint of uneasiness in his eyes.

"We were going to give you a chance to provide insight into the story. It will go on without you—and we'll note that Dunning was uncooperative. People will come to their own conclusions about why," Owen said with a shrug.

Owen understood the man's reticence to talk with reporters, but the missing bodies story had gotten a lot of press and was practically tailor-made for gossip.

The man swallowed like a gigged fish, managing to look even more pale. "I don't know anything about missing bodies."

"You're in charge, aren't you?" Calvin cocked his head inquisitively. "Even if it didn't happen on your watch, you should get reports, right?"

"I'm not here twenty-four hours a day," he protested. "This is a big complex. People come and go. When a death happens, the body is brought here. The next shift takes care of it. We only have one person on staff at night. They can't be everywhere at once."

"And no one told you that five bodies have been reported missing in the last two months?" Owen picked up the questions.

The coroner wiped a hand across his sweaty forehead. "Maybe. It gets busy here. What was I supposed to do about it? Cops don't care any more than the families do."

The man's complete lack of concern for the humanity of the hospital's patients made Owen angry, forcing him to tamp down on his reaction before he took a swing at the coroner.

"How about launching an internal investigation to figure out who is stealing corpses?" Owen replied. "Did you even ask around? Or did you figure someone did you a favor because there were five fewer bodies to bury?" He hoped his pointed comment would goad the coroner into saying more than he intended.

"A janitor got fired, so I heard. Didn't know the man. He worked the night shift. That's all I heard. Why he did it and what became of the bodies, I have no idea," the man retorted. "Now get out of my morgue."

"Thank you for your time," Calvin said as they departed, managing a civil tone that Owen couldn't have mustered.

They didn't speak until after they were in the carriage, and Winston headed out of the institution's gates.

"Well, that was interesting," Owen said in a tart tone.

Calvin gave a dark chuckle. "I guess you can call it that. There wasn't anything handy for me to read by touch except the mortuary tools, and that's a hard no." He shivered. "The coroner certainly didn't give a damn about the missing bodies until he realized the situation might reflect badly on him. Do you think he's involved?"

Owen paused to think for a moment, then shook his head. "No—he's too lazy. He might accept a bribe to look the other way or be out of the morgue at a particular time so the theft could happen, but he doesn't strike me as industrious enough to come up with the scheme himself."

"Hmm. I guess you're right. It's bad enough that he's like that at Dunning, where no one seems to give a rat's ass about the patients, but I hope he isn't the standard for hospital morgues," Calvin replied, his feelings clear in his tone.

"Not that it's an excuse, but I would imagine that to be a tough job for someone with empathy," Owen grudgingly admitted.

"Your patients aren't ever going to get better. At most you can bring closure. When the families are involved, that might be gratifying, feeling that you helped them let go. But a place like Dunning? How do you work somewhere that houses one thousand people no one cares about? I'd think you'd have to learn not to care as well, or it would be overwhelmingly depressing," Owen said.

Calvin took his hand, threading their fingers together, and let their knees bump in a gesture of reassurance. "All the more reason for us to get to the bottom of the thefts. And we will."

Owen squeezed Calvin's hand, appreciating the support.

"It was like that back in Boston…" Calvin looked out the window instead of at Owen. He rarely spoke about his rough younger days, and Owen watched him closely as he talked. "People talk about how awful the street gangs were—and they definitely were bad—but the gangs formed because no one else cared.

"The cops couldn't be bothered, so when there were thefts, or someone got beat up, the gangs handled it. But no one hears about how they got food to people who were hungry or took up a collection if someone needed medicine," Calvin went on. "The Church didn't take care of everyone, especially the people it didn't consider to be deserving. Neither did the aid societies. We did what we could."

Even if the money passed on as charity was stolen. Like they say, needs must when the devil drives.

Owen looked at their joined hands, running his thumb over Calvin's enlarged knuckles. Calvin flinched. Owen understood. No matter how much he dressed up or how fine his clothing, one look at his hands marked him as a brawler. That was another reason Calvin fancied thin leather gloves in the winter, which hid his damaged hands and helped him avoid getting a psychic reading from everything he touched.

"Had to learn to hold my own in the gang. At least when I went into the Army, I knew how to fight. By the time I came back, a lot of the guys I ran with were dead or in jail. I was lucky my father gave me an ultimatum about going into the military, or I probably would have gone the same way," Calvin added.

Owen raised their hands and pressed a kiss to Calvin's. "I'm glad you got out. You did the best you could with the cards you were dealt. There's no shame in that."

"Not to you, and that's one more thing I love about you," Calvin replied. "But a lot of other people aren't so charitable. I was lucky I didn't have an arrest record when I mustered in. I deserved one—I just didn't get caught."

Owen watched Calvin closely. "What you saw growing up, it helps you see those patients at Dunning as people. That's a good thing to come out of a bad situation."

Calvin sighed and squeezed Owen's hand again. "I guess so. But it makes it all the harder to get to the bottom of the thefts when the cops and authorities aren't going to care more than that coroner did. They don't want the bad headlines, so they'll have to look like they're doing something, but if it weren't for that, they wouldn't bother."

"Then we'll embarrass them into it with the help of our *muckraking* reporter friends." Owen tried to cheer Calvin. "Get them to do right in spite of themselves."

The Dunning campus sprawled over one hundred and sixty acres. That included the poor farm where residents grew crops as well as space for the buildings and a large cemetery to accommodate the dead no one else claimed.

"The cemetery serves the whole county," Owen pointed out as Winston pulled up to the modest gates. Unlike the large stone entranceways at Chicago's private cemeteries, the Cook County Cemetery had two brick pillars with a wrought iron sign between them, probably erected with labor from the residents.

"All of the other hospitals, foundling homes, and halfway houses send their unclaimed dead to be buried here, as well as the Dunning corpses," he added, remembering his research. "They might not be quite as fresh as stealing them out of the morgue, but there have been several recent graveyard thefts as well, so whoever wants the bodies doesn't care."

Calvin frowned, looking out the carriage window. "No headstones or mausoleums—or statues. Not even a cross or an angel. Hardly any trees or bushes. It's just empty. That's sad."

"I imagine there are plot records somewhere—but maybe not," Owen said. "For the John Does, there's no name to record. The Tuberculosis sanitarium probably used mass graves at the worst of the plague." The emptiness of the cemetery seemed a final indignity, making the plight of those buried here even more stark.

"I'd hope that even grave robbers have higher standards than taking plague bodies," Calvin replied, wrinkling his nose. "I can't imagine they'd be good for anything. Certainly not for stealing parts to reuse, if we're right about that."

"Let's walk around and see if we can spot recently disturbed graves," Owen said. "There should at least be records to indicate when new bodies are interred. If it's not in the records—it's unofficial and probably a robbery."

Another carriage pulled in behind them. Calvin and Owen exchanged a glance. Up front, Winston shifted so that one hand was on the gun beneath his cloak.

Owen nodded and opened his door as Calvin did the same. Four cops spilled out of the other carriage.

"How can we help you, officers?" Owen came around to stand

beside Calvin. Winston slid to one side, no doubt to have a better shot if it came to violence.

"Heard you were causing trouble at Dunning. You're still on their property. You aren't welcome. Leave," the man in front, a burly bloke with a boxer's handlebar mustache ordered.

"We wanted to pay our respects to the departed," Calvin said. "The cemetery is open to the public for that purpose."

"Troublemaker reporters excluded," the man said, and the other three officers moved to flank him.

"How about government agents?" Owen's voice grew frosty. "Because we're Secret Service."

"Bullshit," the tall man spat.

"We've got badges—and a direct telegraph connection to the Department of the Treasury in Washington, D.C." Owen's calm seemed to fluster the man as Owen slowly reached into his vest pocket and brandished his badge.

"One telegram and this area will be swarming with agents who will turn over every stone to figure out what you're hiding. Probably haul your chief back to Washington to interrogate him. I'm sure he'll be very happy with you when he gets back," Owen said.

"They know we came to Dunning today," Calvin added. "If we don't check in on time, they'll come looking."

That part was fiction, but Owen would have bet money Mustache Cop didn't have a clue. It also was designed to make him think twice if he thought the easy answer was just shooting them and burying them on site.

"We want to drive through the cemetery and see the grounds," Owen said. "Shouldn't take more than a few minutes. You and your boys can wait right there and watch us. Or...we send that telegram, and the next thing you know, there'll be government agents crawling all over the hospital and the grounds, asking awkward questions. Your choice."

Mustache Cop looked like he had an ulcer. "Fine. We'll watch you —and then you leave and never come back."

"Pleasure talking with you," Owen said. He and Calvin made sure they didn't turn their backs as they got into the carriage, and Winston's stance suggested he had his gun trained on the cops the whole time beneath his cloak.

"What do you make of that?" Calvin asked as they drove farther into the cemetery, following the circular road that took them around the perimeter.

"I figure the coroner raised an alarm, and someone higher up panicked," Owen answered. They could see the cops standing beside their carriage, not moving out of position.

"Think they were going to jump us?"

"Wouldn't be surprised if that was their plan. I didn't want to mention the Secret Service just yet, but I figured it beat being shot and buried in an unmarked grave," Owen said.

Calvin shuddered, and Owen placed his hand on his arm to steady him. "I wasn't going to let that happen," Owen assured him.

"I knew folks back in Boston who had no family to claim their bodies and ended up in the Potter's field. At the worst of times, I thought I might too," Calvin admitted.

"Those days are over." Owen leaned toward him to meet his eyes, emphasizing his point. "That's not something you need to worry about. Our work is dangerous, but we have friends and the family we've made of them. You're not alone, and I'll do everything in my power to keep you from ever being alone again."

They finished their circuit of the cemetery and drove past the cops, who glowered as they passed but did not try to interfere.

When they returned to the stable, Calvin and Owen climbed down from the carriage.

"I'll return the horses and the rig," Winston told them. "And I'll check on our horses while I'm there. It's a short walk back to the train from here. I'll meet you there."

They traveled with three riding horses, which were stabled while they were stationary for any length of time. Owen knew that Winston ensured the horses had better accommodations than most human travelers and appreciated his care.

Owen kept a sharp eye out, but it didn't look like the Dunning administration had sent any additional cops after them. Then again, he didn't know how the police would have known where to look since he and Calvin hadn't provided their names, let alone the location of their train car.

The train station was just around the corner, quiet this time of day. Owen startled when the ghost he had asked to keep an eye on the car popped up in front of him, and Owen put a hand out to stop Calvin.

"What?"

"Ghost." Owen listened to his spectral snitch. "Several men have been watching the Pullman all day. They haven't tried to get in, but they don't have a reason to hang around." He silently thanked the spirit as footsteps sounded nearby.

"Don't run." A man's voice came from behind them. "We just want to talk."

"An invitation delivered by messenger is the usual process," Calvin observed in a dry tone.

"Yeah, well. Witches do things their way," the man answered. "We're going up the street to Barone's Restaurant. They've got the back room ready for us. Don't cause a ruckus, and you'll be on your way in no time."

The ghosts had vanished, making Owen wonder who the witch was and why the spirits had fled. He and Calvin exchanged a look, weighing the odds of putting up a fight. Meeting in a public place made it less likely that the men simply wanted to kill them, Owen thought.

Then again, he'd been wrong before.

Owen wondered if they would encounter Winston on their way or if he would see them and realize something was wrong, but they did not cross paths with their valet. That made him worry that Winston might have been waylaid. Winston could hold his own in a fight, but whoever wanted a word with them seemed to have brought a small army. That suggested one thing.

Chicago Mob.

Chapter 3
Calvin

Barone's Restaurant was a tidy family-run establishment tucked into a quiet side street. Neat lettering on the windows advertised homemade sauces and pasta, pastries, and veal on Sundays. The aroma of onions, garlic, and fresh tomatoes made Calvin's stomach rumble when they walked inside.

Wooden wainscoting, a pressed tin ceiling, and a checkerboard tile floor suggested that the restaurant had been around for a long time. In the back, Calvin caught a glimpse of brass fixtures and the mirrored backsplash of a bar.

"We have a private room. We're friends with the owner," the man said.

An older woman with gray hair and a matronly dark blue dress nodded to them and returned to wiping off tables. The other workers paid them no mind. Whoever the toughs were who brought them here, the restaurant staff didn't seem to be afraid.

Maybe the gangsters are part of the family too.

Calvin and Owen walked shoulder to shoulder down the hallway toward the bar, and he finally caught a glimpse of their hosts in the large backbar mirror. Four dark-haired men followed them, all muscular and rough. Calvin felt certain they had guns, and even though no one had tried to take his weapon, the odds weren't good for a fight in close quarters, especially with civilians nearby.

They want to talk? We'll talk.

A young busboy ushered them into a private dining room. No food or drink on the table suggested this would be a short meeting. At least, Calvin hoped that was the meaning.

Calvin sized up their hosts with the seasoned eye from his wild days. These men seemed a little too old and a bit too organized to be mere gang members, which lent credence to the mobster theory. Oddly, that made him feel a little better about their situation.

One of the bodyguards gestured for Calvin and Owen to sit. A man about Calvin's height with Macassared hair and an aura of authority sat across from them. Two guards stood on either side.

"What brings the feds to Chicago this time?" he asked.

Word travels fast. Did he hear from the cops, or did someone track our Pullman car?

"Official business," Calvin replied pleasantly, not wanting to make it too easy. The look he and Owen traded confirmed they were both of the same mind, to see what information they could get from the mobster while giving up as little themselves as they could.

"You can do better than that." Their host's smile didn't reach his eyes. "Here. A gesture of goodwill. My name is Luca Conti. I am head of security for the Conti and Bianchi families. I take my job very seriously. We like things to stay very quiet, and we take care of our own problems. So...Agents Sharps and Springfield—what brings you to Chicago?"

When they got out of here—*if* they got out—Calvin was going to talk to Winston about how Conti could have found out what he knew. But first, Calvin weighed stonewalling versus laying his cards on the table. A glance from Owen told him his partner would follow his lead, whatever he chose.

"We're here because of all the missing bodies. Too many have been stolen to just be supplying medical schools," Calvin said. "We want to find out who's taking them and what's being done with the corpses."

Of all the answers Calvin could have given, the truth seemed to set

Conti back on his heels. Calvin imagined Conti knew of other illegal goings-on that might have drawn attention, and the surprise showed in his face.

"I am involved in many business ventures throughout this side of the city. That usually keeps me well informed. I did not realize we had an epidemic of dead people walking away," Conti replied, likely using humor to cover being surprised.

"We doubt they're walking," Owen spoke up. "Most are taken before they're even buried. They've been vanishing from hospitals, settlement houses, and the county morgue. People no one would usually miss. But someone has a reason for taking them, and our bosses want to know what that is."

Conti remained quiet for a moment, with a look that suggested he was taking them seriously. "So what? They're dead, and they don't have families, or their families aren't involved. If no one cares—why do you? I understand the disrespect, but where's the harm?"

"He's worried about the magic."

They turned to see an old woman in a black dress framed in the doorway. Dark hair piled atop her head framed a thin face with high cheekbones and alert brown eyes. Owen nudged his leg under the table, and Calvin guessed his thoughts.

Strega. *Witch.* "Mrs. Bianchi," Conti acknowledged the newcomer for their sake.

"Yes, ma'am," Calvin replied as Owen nodded. "We just can't figure out why someone with magic wants the bodies—and that's a worry."

"Fi." She pretended to spit to one side. Calvin had to listen closely to catch her words in her thick accent. "Nothing good. I lay spells to protect the dead in our neighborhood for that reason. Someone is doing death magic—very dark but powerful. It is an abomination."

"Have you heard anything? Rumors spread fast," Calvin asked. If the Conti-Bianchi mafia family could be an asset, Calvin had struck worse deals.

One of the bodyguards leaned down to whisper something to Conti, who nodded.

"Apparently, there has been talk, but since it didn't affect our territory or our people, I hadn't heard it. I will ask my people to keep their ears open after this," Conti said with a note of reproof that clearly landed on his subordinates.

"I know the covens," Mrs. Bianchi said. "The Family witches and the ones who are not part of our business. This does not sound like their doing, but I will inquire." She gave Calvin a pointed look.

"If someone is taking corpses to use them and not just sell them like the body snatchers did, then this is something we should watch closely." She directed her comments to Conti, and it had the feel of an order. Conti didn't flinch, but his acceptance was clear.

Interesting. Conti is clearly top dog with his Mob family, but he listens to the strega.

"It appears we have a common interest," Conti said. "We will keep the people under our protection safe, and I will make sure I'm kept aware."

"If your research turns up anything that might help our investigation, we would appreciate an update," Calvin said.

Conti seemed to find that amusing. "Of course. And I trust you gentlemen will do the same."

Calvin took it as the polite throwdown that it was.

"Of course." His tone and frozen smile matched Conti's.

Conti leaned forward. "I am quite serious. If one of my *family* is involved, it is up to me to mete out a punishment. I don't recognize the government's authority in such areas."

"And see, the government feels the same way about you," Owen said. "So here we are. Let's agree that stopping the thefts and whatever scheme is behind them is a common interest and leave the punishing to whoever gets to the criminals first."

Conti's smile didn't reach his eyes. "As you wish."

If the body snatching involved some of Conti's people working a side angle gone bad, Calvin didn't doubt that the Mob boss would deal with the perpetrators more harshly than the law allowed. If it was an operation rooted in strife between mafia families, Calvin preferred to stay out of the line of fire so long as the problem was handled.

And if the Mob boss changed his mind about benefiting from the thefts, Calvin and Owen would deal with the situation.

"I'd offer you dinner, but I suspect it would run afoul of your tiresome rules and regulations," Conti said with a slight smile that made it clear he enjoyed needling them. "If you're ever looking for a good meal on your own dime, there's nowhere better than Barone's."

"We will keep that in mind," Owen said.

Knowing how much his partner loved good Italian food, Calvin suspected they would be sampling the fare at some point during their visit to Chicago.

"You're free to go." Conti gave a magnanimous sweep of his hand. "I wish you good hunting."

Calvin and Owen stood, and Calvin paused. "While we always appreciate tips and assistance, the surest way to flood Chicago with feds is to get in our way. Just so we're clear."

Conti's smile flattened. "Crystal."

Calvin and Owen walked out like they weren't turning their backs on a half dozen armed mobsters. No one tried to stop them, and Calvin's stomach growled traitorously as they walked back through the restaurant to the door.

They waited to talk until they were out of sight of Barone's and nearly to the Pullman. Calvin looked around to ensure that none of Conti's toughs had followed them, although that didn't rule out unknown informants. Owen swept the area for ghosts and magic now that they knew a witch was involved.

"Well, that was interesting," Calvin observed.

"Are you surprised? This *is* Chicago," Owen replied.

"Not really. But I'd prefer it not to turn into a Mafia war between families—or covens."

"That could get...messy."

Calvin felt a sense of relief that he interpreted as meaning he had crossed their protective wards as they stepped into the Pullman car.

"I trust everything is all right?" Winston asked, which was as close as he would ever admit to being alarmed at their sudden absence.

"We had a little heart-to-heart with the local Mob boss." Owen hung up his coat as Calvin went to do the same. The air smelled of fresh coffee and roasting meat for dinner. "He claims they're not involved, but he'll look into it—without us. Oh, and there are witches."

"Because, of course, there are," Calvin muttered. Good witches were one thing. Dark witches who abused their power made him angry on general principle.

He figured the verdict was out on what camp Nonna Bianchi fell into, depending on her involvement. He would prefer her to be an ally, but they had other friends and resources if circumstances proved otherwise.

"Come in, have a hot coffee, and get warmed up," Winston told them. "Dinner is in the oven. I have some news as well. Go sit in the parlor—I'll bring the drinks to you."

Several new newspapers awaited them as they settled on the tufted velvet couch. Despite the chill outside, the train car was comfortably warm.

"Here you go." Winston bustled in with a tray. "This should take the chill off."

Calvin's first sip assured him that whiskey had been added to the coffee, no doubt for medicinal purposes.

"Hits the spot. Thank you, Winston," Owen said.

Winston set the tray on a side table and sat across from them. "You weren't gone very long, but it was enough time for me to discover a few interesting things."

"More interesting than getting thrown out of a cemetery and cornered by the Mob?" Owen teased.

"You can be the judge. There was a telegram waiting from Miss Tarbell when I came back to the car. She is sending one of her contacts to us tonight, a Miss Abby Edwards, reporter for *The Chicago Tribune*," Winston replied with a cat-that-ate-the-canary smile. "Whom Miss Tarbell said is *very* well-connected with people we should meet."

Ida Tarbell was a firebrand journalist and reformer who wasn't afraid to take on targets like Standard Oil. That made her a hero in some circles and a dangerous nuisance in others. Given her extensive network of contacts and penchant for research, she had been a big help to Calvin and Owen in previous cases they had worked on before teaming up.

"How is she? It's been a while since I've heard from her. I hope she's causing the right kind of trouble," Calvin said.

"I will look up mentions of her in the newspapers the next time I visit a library," Winston promised. "She is, indeed, an extraordinary woman."

"Did the telegram say what was so *interesting* about Abby Edwards?" Owen savored his spiked coffee.

"No, but judging from her column in today's *Tribune*, she has strong opinions on the desecration of graves and society's utter lack of concern for the mortal remains of the less fortunate," Winston replied in a wry tone.

"Do we have a way to set an appointment with Miss Edwards?" Calvin asked.

Winston checked his watch. "She should be here in half an hour. I've invited her to dine with us."

IN EXACTLY THIRTY MINUTES, a knock came at the Pullman's door. Winston went to answer and welcomed their visitor, standing aside for her to enter.

"Mr. Calvin Springfield, Mr. Owen Sharps, may I present Miss Abby Edwards."

Abby Edwards looked to be in her late thirties, a handsome woman with a knot of brown hair and a strong chin. Intelligence glittered in her blue eyes, and her gaze seemed to take in the men and their surroundings with the thoroughness Calvin expected of a seasoned reporter.

"Pleased to meet you." She turned to thank Winston, then moved to shake hands with Calvin and Owen. "Happy to make your acquaintance."

"Please, come in," Calvin invited.

"May I bring you tea or coffee?" Winston asked.

"Tea, please," she replied with a smile. "That would be wonderful. It's gotten quite cool outside."

Winston led them into the parlor and Abby took a seat in the wing chair, sitting primly with perfect posture.

"Please pass along our best wishes and thanks to Miss Tarbell," Calvin said. "We have enjoyed working with her and hope she is doing well."

Abby smiled, which softened her features and brought an unexpected glint of merriment to her eyes. "I will. She's a good friend—and a wonderful colleague. We write to each other often."

"How can we be of help?" Owen and Calvin sat on the sofa facing Abby. With company, they maintained a respectable distance between them. Winston slipped out to bring tea for them, returning quickly with three steaming cups.

"I've been at the *Tribune* for three years now," Abby said. "I started on the society page and fought my way out to write for the opinion section as well as cover news stories. A friend of mine, Molly Dawson, runs a settlement house. Are you familiar with the concept?"

Both Calvin and Owen nodded, which seemed to surprise Abby. "Good. Less explaining. Molly confided to me that she has heard about the bodies of people who died during the night vanishing.

"That made her keep her ears open to what some of their residents and visitors were talking about. More than once, people commented on the bodies of street people who died disappearing before the police could come to take them away," Abby added.

She paused to sip her tea, and the momentary look of bliss at the good flavor softened the intensity of her expression. Calvin got the impression Abby was highly intelligent, relentless in pursuit of a story, and unafraid to ruffle feathers for a good cause.

He liked her already.

"Molly started making inquiries. She can be fearless when something sets her off," Abby said in a fond tone, making it clear she approved. "Then I heard about the explosion—and the missing body. A tragedy, and I suspect, not an accident."

"Oh?" Calvin was intrigued to see how she had arrived at the same conclusion he and Owen held.

"I knew Marvin Cobb, the man who disappeared," she said.

"We were told he was a reporter—and was also looking into the missing bodies," Owen said.

Abby nodded. "We were working on the story from different angles for different papers, but it was a friendly competition. Marvin was a good man, and he didn't deserve what happened to him."

Calvin frowned. "We don't believe the gas leak was an accident. If you're investigating the missing bodies, then you're in danger too."

"I realize that. Which is why I hired my brother to be my driver and bodyguard until this all settles down. But I refuse to be scared off the story. The fact that someone is willing to kill for it tells me there's more here than hard-luck men selling corpses to medical schools."

Calvin had to admire her pluck. *She'd have made a good agent.*

Victorian social conventions restricted the role of women, but clever—and stubborn—individuals found ways around the rules or crashed through them by dint of sheer force of personality.

Calvin and Owen had a number of female friends whose aid proved essential in their cases. If they suspected what Calvin and Owen were to each other or even their leanings, it didn't seem to bother them.

"I've spoken to his family, offering condolences, and they are bereft," she went on. "I don't believe it was an accident either. My suspicion is that whoever killed him thought it would be a final indignity to take his corpse, and they counted on the fire to hide the evidence."

Calvin and Owen nodded in agreement.

"That's what we suspect as well," Owen said. "Have you turned up any ideas about what's being done with the bodies since they aren't being stolen in the usual way?"

Abby paused. "Do you believe in the unseen?"

"You mean ghosts? Magic? The paranormal?" Owen asked. He and Calvin didn't admit to their abilities to outsiders, but they often tapped the skills of other psychics and witches in their cases.

"Yes," she replied and looked braced for reproof or even laughter.

"We do," Calvin replied cautiously. "Some people are charlatans, but real abilities exist."

She let out a breath and relaxed a bit more. "Good. Because I'm compiling evidence that what's going on is a combination of witchcraft —and science."

Calvin cocked his head, curious. "We've been wondering whether the science part involves galvanism. Not something as outlandish as in that British author's book—"

"*Frankenstein*, by Mary Shelley," Abby said, and Calvin nodded.

"Yes. Not bringing a corpse back to life or stitching a whole person together from pieces of other bodies," he clarified. "But robbing the dead for parts. Transplants have been done on living people. What if someone wanted to go looking for replacements to heal wealthy patients—hearts, spleens, livers? A missing hand or foot? Or maybe, for someone desperate to avoid detection, faces?"

The ghoulish topic wasn't proper pre-dinner conversation, but Abby didn't seem to mind.

"I like the way you think," she said with a conspiratorial smile. "I don't know that Mr. Cobb's imagination went in that direction, but it's something that occurred to me as well. I quite liked that book, although the premise was terrifying."

"I'm something of a fan of horror novels," Owen confessed. "I thought the book was well done."

"I shouldn't admit such things, but so am I." She dropped her voice. "It's not considered ladylike." Her smile suggested how little she cared about convention.

"Dinner is ready," Winston said from the parlor doorway.

By unspoken agreement, they left aside the ghastly topics of missing bodies and cadaver pieces. The topics ranged from the war with Spain to the Antarctic expedition to local events. Abby recounted her memories of the World's Fair just a few years prior, proving to be a lively conversationalist.

After dinner, over more coffee, they made plans.

"I'll see if my friend has heard more from her settlement house contacts," Abby said. "I've made a few friends who are psychics and mediums. I'll ask them as well. I don't know any witches, but my friends do—reputable ones. This should be very interesting."

"The Mob may be paying close attention." Owen gave an abbreviated recap of their meeting with Conti without mentioning names. "Watch your step."

"I always do," she said with a laugh that countered her serious manner.

"We have contacts with the Pinkertons and other agents in the area," Calvin said. "We'll see what they've heard on the grapevine and share what we learn. I suspect some of our friends also know people in the local covens—I'm hoping we can get some insights."

Calvin felt sure Winston had already put out feelers to others in the witch community. He was especially curious to see what role the Mob witches played.

By the time Abby's brother knocked at the door to escort her to their carriage, they had made plans to meet again in two days and exchange leads. Calvin closed the door behind her and turned back to Owen.

"Good to know someone else came to similar conclusions, right?"

Owen ran a hand back through his hair. "Right—in an ominous sort of way. I'd feel better if she had solid evidence that dismissed the whole thing as a misunderstanding. I have a feeling this is going to be messy."

They had a nightcap in the parlor and finished reading the newspapers, remarking to each other over sports scores and humorous stories of people doing odd things.

Most items didn't trigger Calvin's magic unless they had a strong emotional connection to a person or to something that happened. That saved him from needing his gloves all the time and being bombarded by images. Over time, Calvin had gained control as well, making it possible to heighten a faint link or tamp down one that was too strong.

"Unless you have need of something, I'm going to make an early night of it," Winston said, leaning into the compartment. "I sent messages to some friends of mine in the supernatural community in town, but it may take a day or two for me to hear back. If we're lucky, they might give us some clarity about where the local covens stand and who is aligned with whom."

"Thank you," Calvin said. "For everything."

"You are most welcome. Have a good evening."

Since it seemed early to turn in just yet, Calvin and Owen settled on the sofa once more, sitting hip to knee now that there was no one to interrupt.

"Did you see there's a Wild West show coming to Chicago this week?" Calvin turned his paper so Owen could see the illustrated, full-page advertisement.

"Huh. I heard that the Western show during the World's Fair was one of the biggest ever," Owen remarked.

"How do you think it compares to what you saw when you were out there?" Calvin asked. He and Owen had talked about the years before they met, but rarely in great detail since it seemed as if they had been in constant danger. Seeing the ad for the show, Calvin tried to picture Owen as a cowboy and found the image surprisingly sexy.

"I suspect it's highly sensationalized, much less dangerous, and the performers bathe more regularly," Owen replied in a droll tone. "I was with the Army, not a cowboy, although we ran into them from time to time, especially on leave in town."

"With all the riding, sharpshooting, rodeo, and historical recreations, it sounds like a very manly man's sort of show," Calvin remarked. He had little patience for men who needed to prove their masculinity by trying to outdo everyone around them with dangerous stunts.

Owen snickered. "If only they knew. No one talked about it, but it wasn't unusual for men on long cattle drives to pair up for the duration since they could go months without sight of a woman. Some didn't mind that part at all—I think they signed on because of it, to tell the truth."

Calvin raised an eyebrow. "Really?"

Owen nodded. "It's not the kind of thing they reported in the newspapers back East, where stories about the tough-as-nails cowboy sold copies, but it's true. For some men, they paired up for one drive and went their separate ways like it never happened when they finished the job. For others, the ones who were lifers, they were true mates, good as married but without the paperwork. A few even got rings."

"And they didn't get lynched?" Calvin had never heard this side of the story.

Owen shrugged. "They were careful. Certainly didn't parade around town. Knew who to trust and who to avoid. But it was a pretty open secret, from what I saw."

"Was it like that in the Army too?" Calvin wasn't sure he wanted to know, but he had to ask.

Owen hesitated before answering. "Not exactly. Being with a man wasn't technically against military law. People who got caught could still end up discharged—but not thrown in jail. From what I saw, it varied.

"Some of it was whether the commanding officer chose to look the other way. Relatively small, close-knit groups on extended missions often formed pairs because the open range is a lonely place," Owen replied. "Although the brass would never have admitted it, I think they preferred fucking to drinking and shooting up the local outpost."

"Did you—" Calvin didn't finish his question.

Owen was quiet again. "I knew my interests from the time I hit puberty, and I knew not to say anything or act on them in the polite, Christian, Southern society where I was raised."

He looked off into the distance, pointedly not making eye contact with Calvin. "I picked up the basics of how it was for men with women from hearing people talk and growing up on a farm, but didn't have much to go on when it came to two men together.

"I could guess it involved touching. I'd figured that part out early for myself and there were a few hurried fumbles in the back of the barn or a bathroom, but I didn't have any idea there were other ways to satisfy each other until I went West. I was young, and there were older men happy to contribute to my education," Owen said.

He turned to meet Calvin's gaze. "There was never anyone serious, anyone who wasn't just a good time for an evening. No one who mattered. Nothing like what we are to each other."

Calvin believed him, although the idea that such things had been tacitly ignored, if not exactly accepted, surprised him. The jealousy that flared when he thought about Owen with anyone else caught him off guard with its heat, even though he trusted Owen completely and knew how much he valued their bond.

Calvin pushed those thoughts aside and managed his sexiest smile. "Want to give me a private demonstration of ridin' and ropin', cowboy?"

"I think that sounds like a fine way to end the evening," Owen agreed with a grin that made his hunger clear. "Let's head to bed."

Once the door closed, Calvin pushed Owen against the wall, pressing their bodies together and grinding their cocks against each other through their trousers. Calvin could feel Owen's stiff prick and loved his soft groan as their kisses turned hungry.

"Clothing. Off," Owen said when he broke away for a gasp of air. They made short work of buttons and collars, leaving a trail of shirts, pants, socks, and silk drawers as they wrestled to the bed. They took their time exploring with fingertips and lips, gliding palms across skin, taking in the taste and scent.

Calvin ran his hands through Owen's hair, cupped his cheek, and kissed him slow and deep. Owen shifted to wrap his body around Calvin, rubbing their cocks together.

Owen kissed Calvin again with passion.

"I love you," he murmured. "Only, ever, you. Don't worry about my past. No one holds a candle to you."

Calvin returned the kiss, tender and lingering. "Love you too. Always."

No matter how many times they made love, Calvin was always hungry for more. Before Owen, most of Calvin's experience lay in anonymous fumbling in dark corners or city bathhouses. He rarely had the safety or the luxury of time to explore and savor, and those random partners hadn't been worth the risk. His one serious boyfriend ended up murdered, which had driven Calvin back into the closet until he met Owen.

Maybe it was Owen's time out West, where men who spent long stretches of time riding the range held to different behaviors than back East. Owen was comfortable with his desire while still being cautious.

"How do you want it?" Owen breathed next to Calvin's ear. His hand went to Calvin's already-hard cock, giving it a stroke or two that earned a moan from Calvin.

"Want to feel you in me," Calvin murmured. "Take our time."

Once their new case started, leisurely evenings were few and far between. Calvin hungered for release, but also for a memory to carry him through until time was once more on their side.

"Sounds good to me." Owen kissed him, sliding his tongue between Calvin's lips and plundering his mouth.

They fell together and lingered in a tangled pile to explore with hands and mouths and tongues. A quick fuck took the edge off, but Calvin had learned to appreciate how satisfying making love could be with time and safety, reaching their peak over and over again, increasing in intensity until the pleasure was nearly too much to bear.

They usually took turns being top and bottom, depending on mood. Tonight, Calvin wanted to feel Owen's weight above him, hard cock driving into Calvin's ass and leaving him pleasantly sore in the morning, a reminder of who he belonged to.

Dangerous work left few illusions. Calvin knew that a stray bullet could tear them apart forever, and that knowledge made him even hungrier, desperate to show Owen how much he cared and to sate himself with Owen's body.

"Ride me, cowboy," Calvin murmured.

"Gotta get you ready first." Owen slicked his fingers with a generous portion of Vaseline from the container in the bedside stand, teasing at Calvin's taint and tight hole. "Then I'm going to give you a fucking you won't forget."

Calvin drew his ankles up to his hips and spread his legs wide, offering himself completely to Owen.

"God, the way you look when you do that," Owen whispered. "All for me, so ready."

"Always for you," Calvin breathed. "Only you."

Owen leaned forward, licking Calvin's cock as he worked first one finger and then two more into his pucker. The intrusion made Calvin's hard-on flag, but he began to plump up once more as Owen took him into his mouth, licking and sucking as his fingers gradually opened Calvin up.

When Owen twisted just so and hit that magic spot, Calvin arched and had to bite at the pillow to stay quiet as he came, jetting his release into Owen's willing mouth.

When Calvin dropped back to the mattress, Owen sat on his heels, licking his lips like the Cheshire Cat. He didn't wait to move forward, bringing Calvin's legs onto his shoulders and pressing his rock-hard cock into Calvin's ass until he was fully seated inside.

"So good," Calvin whispered. "Love to feel you."

"Feels pretty damn good to me, too," Owen assured him. He kissed Calvin, letting him taste himself on his lips, then slid back and forward again.

Calvin loved to feel the slide of Owen's sweat-soaked skin against his own, the heat of his breath on Calvin's neck, the intimacy of Owen's tongue on sensitive spots. He felt his second climax rise and overtake him, making him shake at every touch. Owen came seconds later, claiming Calvin with his muscular body.

When they finally toppled to the side, and Owen slipped out, Calvin gave his lover a sleepy, sated kiss. "That was…perfect."

"Don't say things like that. They'll go to my head," Owen deflected, but Calvin could see he glowed at the praise.

Owen reached for a discarded undershirt to clean them and the wet spot on the sheet and tossed it back on the floor. Calvin rearranged the bedding, and they slipped beneath the covers, facing each other and still close enough to touch.

Later, when they lay tangled up together, and Calvin listened to Owen's breath, he did his best to push all concerns about cowboys and soldiers from his mind, but his dreams were restless.

Chapter 4
Owen

It's good to see you, Louisa," Owen said as a tall, thin woman met them at a tea house near the station.

"It's becoming a habit. St. Louis and now Chicago." She settled across from them. Calvin had obtained a table in a far corner where they could talk without being overheard.

"Yes. Never a dull moment," Calvin added. They were quiet as the server brought cups, hot water, and several flavors of tea as well as honey and lemon. After they had filled their drinks, Owen leaned forward.

"You always know the good gossip."

She chuckled. "That's my job, isn't it?" Louisa might not look like what most people pictured as a Pinkerton agent, but she was a highly skilled, well-trained, and very successful operative. Like them, Louisa's job moved her from city to city depending on the investigation.

"Have you heard anything about the bodies that have gone missing? Or what the local covens are up to?" Owen asked.

Louisa paused to sip her tea. "I'm working in the patent office at the moment, so mostly I see starry-eyed inventors and blueprints for unlikely contraptions. Not a lot of dead bodies, but I've met a technology witch or two."

"A what?" Calvin echoed.

"Someone who tries to combine magic and science, using the magic to fill in the gaps the science hasn't quite figured out," she answered. "Fascinating stuff—and a little scary. They can't come out and call it magic of course, but that's what it is. And they're not popular with the old-school spellcasters, so it's ruffled some feathers in the magical community, so I hear."

"Interesting," Owen replied. "Has it caused enough of a dust-up to start a witch war?"

"There are always big personalities who want to be center stage all the time," Louisa said. "Sometimes they end up leading covens. That's usually bad for the members and everyone else because they're more invested in power and fame than in using magic to accomplish something worthwhile." Her sour tone made her feelings clear.

"I think those types are everywhere," Calvin agreed.

"Oh, they are. But they gravitate toward callings that favor a bit of showmanship," Louisa said. "Theater. Music. Government. And magic, because it's not just what you say and do, it's how it's said and done."

"Good point," Owen acknowledged. "Any new tensions? How about among the Mob families?"

"Always. It wouldn't be Chicago without back-alley fights," Louisa said with a resigned half-smile. "Keeps things interesting. That's not what I was sent to sniff around about, but I'll tell you what I've heard.

"The covens that are from rival Mob families always have spats going. They usually leave everyone else out of it, but sometimes people get caught in the crossfire. The community reacts very badly to that, and the covens go on their best behavior—at least superficially—until people stop paying attention," she added.

"For the other covens, it seems to be bad feelings between the traditionalists and the progressives," Louisa went on. "The traditionalists want everything said in Latin or ancient languages and done exactly the way the old books say. The progressives say magic works just fine in English and that the trappings can be brought into the modern age."

Calvin couldn't hide a smile. "That seems to be the battle in every profession, but I hadn't figured it in witchcraft."

Louisa nodded. "Sad but true. I have a witch friend I can introduce you to. She would know the players much better. Arabella Munson. I'll find a way to put you in touch."

"Much obliged," Calvin replied.

"Back to the missing bodies," Owen said. "Has anyone tried to patent any unusual medical procedures or equipment lately? Especially anything to do with electricity?"

She gave them a shrewd look. "What are you really looking for?"

"We think the theft of fresh bodies isn't about selling them as cadavers for medical schools," Calvin replied. "We've read about doctors wanting to transplant healthy organs for sick ones. Our working theory is that the thieves are selling the bodies for parts that can be attached with some sort of exclusive new technology—or technology magic—that allows them to become replacements for damaged or missing limbs, organs, or even faces."

Louisa took a moment to let that sink in. Her right hand went to clasp a protective bracelet on her left wrist. "You mean like in that Frankenstein book?"

Owen shook his head. "Not exactly. In that book, it was about reanimating the dead. This would be less grandiose—replacing a damaged part—not the whole body."

"The doctor in that book used electricity to bring the creature to life," she mused. "There have been some rather sensational demonstrations of galvanism recently. Dr. Augustus Gordon had a standing-room-only exhibition at the Chicago Coliseum. I'm told that people fainted or threw up at the display."

Owen's eyebrows rose. "What could have been that bad?"

"He had a severed monkey's paw that clenched and unclenched its fist. And a freshly dead calf from one of the slaughterhouses that he got to move in rather ghoulish ways," Louisa shared, looking sick herself. "The newspapers were fascinated and repelled, in equal parts.

Some of them said he was a madman and a danger. Others thought it was the frontier of science. The crowd just loved a show."

Owen retreated behind his cup of tea for a moment while he thought about what she said. "Do you think Gordon is doing off-the-books experiments in his free time?"

Louisa frowned, thinking, then shook her head. "No. He's a veterinarian, not a surgeon. He wouldn't have the knowledge or expertise to do complicated procedures on people."

"Lots of con men have oversold their expertise," Calvin pointed out.

"True. But if there's a whole underground racket going with stolen bodies, there's got to be money behind this. An investor who either sees a way to make a fortune or has some major personal loss that fuels them," she replied. "I've heard Gordon talking with audience members. He can put on a show, but he isn't smart enough to be a con man of the scale it would take to convince people to let him operate on them."

"He's the front man. He might not even know about someone else doing the actual procedures," Owen conjectured.

"I don't think anyone would trust Gordon with that kind of secret," Louisa said. "If he weren't making frog legs twitch, he'd be doing a Vaudeville show somewhere. I wouldn't be surprised if he's an actor pretending to be a doctor."

"Just another snake oil salesman," Calvin replied. "But he's also popularizing the concept and the possibilities of galvanism. Making people comfortable with it. The more they see it, the more normal it seems. That paves the way for a real doctor to quietly offer an expensive, exclusive procedure to select customers."

"That's why they say there's a sucker born every minute," Owen agreed. "Because I'll bet my bottom dollar that there isn't any long-term research on how long a transplant like that might last. When something gets stitched on and starts rotting, they won't be happy."

Louisa scrunched up her face. "Ew."

"Yeah, Owen," Calvin teased. "Watch your words. People are trying to eat." Beneath the table, he bumped Owen's knee in jest.

"There's also an academic, a Dr. Humphries, who has a lecture coming up about transplantation," Louisa told them. "I saw a flyer on a bulletin board. It sounded very theoretical, not splashy, but you might pick up something from watching the audience."

Calvin made sure to write down the details. "Sounds like it could be worth sitting through. Even if Humphries himself isn't involved, there could be someone who is a little too interested hanging around."

They changed subjects after that, sticking to lighter topics. When they finished their tea, Owen and Calvin walked Louisa to her carriage.

"I'll send you a telegram when I know more," Louisa said. "And I'll get something set up with Arabella. In the meantime, watch your backs."

The sunny day and warm temperature tempted them to walk the rest of the way back to the train station. Owen spotted the usual ghosts on the way. The repeaters never changed or noticed anyone. They were just shadows without memory. Several others retained a sense of who they had been and acknowledged Owen.

"There's a man behind you." The tip came from a ghost that looked like he had been a railroad worker in life. *"He's been following you."*

"Ghost says we've got a tail," Owen said under his breath to Calvin.

They exchanged a look and worked the plan they had devised. Owen broke left, Calvin went right, and Owen called out to nearby spirits to hem in their pursuer.

They found a skinny, dark-haired man cowering behind the trash bins, looking like he'd had a fright.

Calvin dragged him up by his collar. "Why were you following us?" Unfortunately, his touch magic worked less reliably on fabric and barely at all skin-to-skin.

"I wasn't—"

"The ghosts say you were," Owen said with a cold smile. "I sent them for you. Want to see them again? Maybe it will help your memory."

"No! Please. Don't," the man protested.

"Why were you following us?"

The man's gaze darted around, and while Owen could feel the presence of the ghosts nearby, they were hiding themselves for now.

"A man said he would pay me. Wanted to know where you went. I'm supposed to meet him and tell him what you did, and he'll give me money," their captive blurted.

"What did he look like?" Calvin demanded.

"Short. Dark hair and dark eyes. Black shirt and pants. Never saw him before. Listen, I don't have anything against you. It's just, I need the money," the man begged.

"Where were you supposed to meet him?" Owen glanced around them. No one seemed to be paying attention.

"Behind the train station in an hour. Look—if you let me go, I'll run in the opposite direction. You'll never see me again, and I won't report in," the man offered.

"But he'll know something's up," Owen said. "And he'll come looking for you. Let's keep your appointment. All of us."

***

THEY ONLY HAD HALF an hour to wait. Owen and Calvin watched from behind the shelter of two stacks of crates while the man paced at the station's cargo entrance. The ghosts remained nearby, just in case.

Owen checked his watch. "He's late."

"Give it time," Calvin said.

Ten minutes later, the contact still hadn't shown up. Their stalker looked ready to panic. By twenty after, Owen figured the man wasn't going to come.

"He stood you up," Owen told the spy. "Or someone stopped him from coming." He took some cash out of his pocket and gave it to the man. "Get as far away from here as you can and don't come back. I don't know what game someone is playing, but you're going to be the loser if you stick around."

"And forget anything you saw about where we were or what we

did," Calvin chimed in. "Make something up if anyone asks. Got that?"

"Yes, sir. Thank you, sir. I'll be on my way." He scrambled to get out of sight, and Owen watched him go.

"What do you think is going to happen?" Calvin asked Owen as they checked their surroundings and headed back to the train.

"Poor bastard is a dead man walking," Owen muttered. "He's seen the contact, so he could recognize whoever sent him after us. The guy who hired him isn't going to want to leave witnesses. I suspect his boss spotted us with him and called off the rendezvous."

"Seems like a lot of bother," Calvin said. "Which side do you think it is? Mobsters or witches?"

"Dunno. It could even be someone involved with grave robbing if they think we're onto them," Owen replied. "We haven't been able to follow the money to guess who's involved in that racket."

They kept walking to the train car, wary of their surroundings but not noticing anything unusual or anyone who paid them particular attention, and reached the Pullman without incident.

"I'm glad Winston put down wardings," Owen said as he felt the familiar frisson when they crossed. "I feel like we're sitting ducks, being in the station and not moving."

"Hard to do our job in Chicago and not actually be *in* Chicago," Calvin replied.

"You know what I meant."

Owen breathed a sigh of relief once they were inside. He didn't know whether the informant would have reported their details to a would-be assassin or whether an unknown player decided to keep track of them, but the uncertainty kept him tense the whole way back.

The car smelled of mulled cider and freshly baked cookies, reminding Owen once again that they had the best attaché ever in Winston. *Plus he's a witch and a good shot. We hit the jackpot.*

"Oh, there you are!" Winston greeted them. "Get settled and I'll bring in your drinks. Dinner won't be ready for a while yet."

Despite the often hectic, dangerous, and unpredictable nature of their lives, Owen cherished the evenings when they could have an unhurried dinner and relax with the newspapers. His younger self wouldn't have been able to comprehend the satisfaction of having a home, a partner, and an unusual but dependable found family.

I didn't know what I was missing. Now that I have this, I'll never let it go.

The apple cider was still steaming when Winston brought in the cups along with a dish of cookies. An envelope lay beside the plate.

"A letter from Miss Edwards came by courier," he told them as he set the tray on a side table. "And I've put out inquiries among the local covens. A few old friends were persuaded to make introductions for me, and as it turned out, there is a witch here I met some time ago."

"Is Arabella Munson one of your contacts?" Calvin asked.

Winston looked surprised. "Yes, actually. She's the witch I met a while back. How do you know her?"

"We don't," Owen said. "But Louisa Sunderson, our Pinkerton contact, wanted to put us in touch with Arabella. So that's a double recommendation."

"I'll see what I can arrange tomorrow," Winston promised. "We still have a little while until dinner. Enjoy the papers, and I'll call you when the food is ready."

They settled in on the couch, closer than appropriate, and sipped their drinks in silence. The apple cider picked up extra flavor from a cinnamon stick, and Owen felt it burn away the chill from outside.

Calvin leaned forward to reach for the note and opened the seal. He scanned it quickly and looked up.

"Well?" Owen asked.

"Miss Edwards wants one of us to come with her tomorrow to meet with Miss Dawson, the woman who runs the settlement house," Calvin said. "That definitely comes through from the resonance I get from the stationery. She apologized for asking for just one, but she thought the both of us might be too intimidating."

"That's fine," Owen said. "I want to see if the ghosts can tell us anything more about the man who was following us. Whoever sent him is likely to try again."

"Maybe Winston can turn something up with his magic," Calvin suggested. "We can ask over dinner."

They leaned back to read the papers and enjoy a moment of not needing to be on guard. Most of the headlines dealt with politics and local issues that weren't important to Owen, but one jumped out at him.

"There was a death at the Wild West Show." Owen turned the page so Calvin could see. "They aren't open yet, so they were setting up, and the performers were practicing," Owen summarized. "One of the riders was thrown from his horse and broke his neck."

Calvin met his eyes. "Are you thinking what I'm thinking?"

"That the body might mysteriously disappear?"

Calvin nodded. "Yeah. Maybe you should have a look while I'm off meeting the settlement lady."

"Okay," Owen agreed, silently glad that if they were going to split up, Calvin's mission for the next day didn't seem likely to be dangerous. "I'll have a look around and see if there's anything strange. Although if the body didn't get snatched, I'll have to come up with another excuse."

"I have faith in you," Calvin joked.

"Dinner is ready." Winston poked his head into the room. "Come to the table."

They sat down to a roast chicken dinner with baked potatoes and vegetables which made Owen's stomach rumble.

"I learned a bit about the warring Mob factions," Winston said as they ate. "Some of it is old news—groups vying for more territory or power among their peers. From what I hear, the two most powerful families are always jockeying for power. It doesn't affect outsiders unless it turns into a shooting war over turf.

"Everyone warned me that a lot of the Chicago cops are on the take, so they look the other way and let the families sort things out on their own," Winston added.

"Lovely. I'd prefer not to get caught in the crossfire," Calvin replied, and Owen nodded in agreement.

"Like with the covens, the older families dominate in more traditional areas—like construction, brothels, and the opium trade," Winston continued. "A few up-and-coming families are betting on new-fangled discoveries like radiation and Tesla coils that aren't proven but *might* turn out to be big."

"What the hell is a Tesla coil?" Owen remembered seeing the name of Nikolai Tesla, the inventor, in the newspaper and had been curious about what he created.

"A way to create very powerful electricity," Calvin replied. At Owen's raised eyebrows, Calvin shrugged.

"Unlike you, I read the whole article, not just the headlines," Calvin replied.

"How powerful?"

"Lightning bolts, according to the reports," Calvin told him.

"Might someone use it for galvanism? Like the lightning in *Frankenstein?*"

"Maybe," Calvin allowed. "There's certainly the possibility that someone would try."

"Looks like we can guess which families the technology witches align with," Owen added.

"Exactly."

"The old-school Mob families stick with prostitution, drugs, bootlegging, racketeering, bars—the usual," Calvin mused. "Maybe even the magically engineered drugs that affect shifters and paranormals. They've all got covens that could figure that stuff out. And the Mobs with more forward-thinking bosses look at replacing body parts for a profit."

"It makes sense," Owen agreed. "But it could be messy as all hell to shut down."

"One step at a time," Calvin cautioned. "If we shut off the supply of new bodies, it gets harder for them to do what they're doing. We need to find more about this showman doing experiments and the guy at the university."

"I will chat with Arabella tomorrow and find a way to make introductions and set up a meeting," Winston said. "In the meantime, please be careful. Witches and the Chicago Mob are a bad combination."

THE NEXT DAY, Calvin and Owen parted with a kiss before they went their separate ways to investigate. Calvin promised a full report of his time with Miss Edwards and the settlement houses, and Owen pledged to fill them in on anything interesting from his investigation at the Wild West Show.

Owen deliberated over how to approach the show. He could go undercover, dressed as a handler, which might get him inside to hear gossip but wouldn't help him connect with the people in charge.

Going in his suit would earn him the derision of the performers but might spook the management into answering his questions. Reluctantly, he decided that dressing like an agent was the better option.

"We're not open to the public yet. Come back next week," the man at the front gate told Owen.

Owen pulled his badge from his inside jacket pocket. "Secret Service. I need to see your head of security."

The worker looked at Owen's badge in consternation. "Wait here." He disappeared into the small building that served as the event office and returned several minutes later with a tall man whose starched collar and gray waistcoat suggested he was management, not one of the performers.

"What appears to be the problem, Agent?" the man said.

"Are you the head of security?" Owen met the man's gaze.

"No, I'm the event manager."

"I need to see the head of security," Owen repeated. "I'd prefer not to need to come back with the police, but asking to speak to your security person is entirely within my purview."

He waited out the manager with a blank expression, letting the other man stew.

Finally, the manager muttered a curse under his breath. "Don't know what good it's going to do, but I'll have someone escort you to the security building. Steven should be there. You need to be accompanied at all times when you're on show property. For your own safety."

"Of course," Owen replied in a neutral voice.

"I'll have Harry walk you over," the manager growled. "If you go wandering off, I'll make sure you get escorted out."

Owen ignored the bluster as Harry, whom he guessed to be a clerk in the show office, walked over.

"Follow me," Harry said with a sheepish smile.

They left the office, and Harry fell into step beside Owen. "Are you really Secret Service?"

Owen nodded. "Yes. Got the badge and everything. By the way, it's illegal to impersonate an agent."

"Oh, I didn't mean anything by it," Harry said. "I just never met someone like that before. I can't imagine what brings you to the show, but I guess it's important—and probably secret."

The security building was a small wooden cabin not far from the show office. The manager could have easily just pointed it out and let Owen find it himself, but clearly he wanted to make his point.

Harry stuck his head into the cabin. "Is Steven here?" Other voices sounded, and Harry opened the door wider and made room for Owen to enter.

A tall, broad-shouldered blond man bustled into the room, took one look at Owen, and paled.

"Owen?"

Owen found himself staring at a ghost from his past who was very much alive. "Hello, Steven."

He knew many men with that first name. It never occurred to Owen that this one would be someone he had served with out West, and during one particularly long, dreary winter, been closer than most friends.

Steven shook off his shock. "Thanks, Harry. I'll take it from here."

Harry looked from one man to the other, clearly figuring that there was a story here he didn't understand. "I'll let the boss know. He's supposed to be escorted everywhere."

Steven gave a curt nod. "I'll make sure of it."

Once Harry left, Steven glanced back at the security office and frowned. "Walk with me, Owen." He clearly didn't want their conversation to be overheard.

"Been a long time." Steven led Owen toward the center ring, where men on horseback practiced their routines for the upcoming show.

"Looks like you did well for yourself after you got out." Owen was genuinely happy that his old friend had found a good position.

"It's a good fit, military background and all," Steven replied. "But look at you. Secret Service?"

Owen shrugged. "Right place, right time, right opportunity. Like you said, it's a good fit."

They were quiet again, listening to the thunder of hoofbeats and the shouts of the riders.

"Did you know I was here?"

Owen shook his head. "No."

"Would you have come if you did?"

Owen was quiet for a moment. "It's business, Steven. I need to know about the man who died. What happened to the body?"

Steven startled. "What do you mean?"

Owen could tell Steven was playing for time to figure out how to react.

"The performer who died—"

"Drew. His name was Drew," Steven said.

Owen nodded. "Was Drew's body stolen?"

Steven's eyes widened. "Jesus, Owen. How the hell did you know that?"

"It's why I'm here in Chicago, investigating a rash of body thefts. The performer would have been a prime corpse and a tempting target," Owen replied.

"Do you know who's doing it? Are you going to bust them?"

"It's a little more complicated," Owen said. "And I can't share details. But it's bigger than one person stealing and selling cadavers. I was hoping you'd have information about who had access and whether anything was disturbed when the body was taken.

"Someone had to get into your compound, know where the body

was being kept, and get out with it," Owen pointed out. "That's a lot for one person on their own. Which tells me that they had help—and might have paid off people with the show to look the other way."

"When Drew got thrown, our show doctor was on scene and pronounced him dead," Steven said. "It was late in the day, so we wrapped him in blankets and took him to the storage shed, figuring we'd call the cops and the coroner in the morning. But when we went to do that, he was gone."

"Was the shed locked?"

"Yes. The lock was picked. Whoever did it scratched it to hell in the process," Steven replied. "Even if it was someone with the show, how did they get a man's body off of the grounds without being seen? And how did a person who works for a traveling show know that there would be someone in town to give the body to?"

"How they moved him without being seen? That wouldn't take a complicated spell. As for how they knew who wanted the body, I suspect the folks involved eyed the show coming to town and figured that with dangerous stunts, something was likely to go wrong. Your people go into town now and again, right? They could meet someone in a bar who made them an offer," Owen said.

"Spells. Like magic?" Steven frowned.

"Yes." Owen waited him out, wondering whether Steven would mock him or consider the possibility.

"And you believe that stuff works?"

"I know it does, if done right." Owen paused. "Are Drew's things still here—clothing, possessions?"

"Probably. I don't imagine anyone's cleaned out his bunk yet."

"Can you take me to it? I might pick up something from his stuff." Owen had never told Steven about his mediumship, but it hadn't really had a reason to come up back in their Army days.

They were silent at first as they walked toward one of several large tents erected behind the fence that separated the public area from the staff section.

"How did you end up with the show?" Owen asked.

Steven shrugged. "When I mustered out, I didn't really have a plan.

But I was good with horses and guns. I went to see the show, and there was a poster looking for security guards. This was about five years ago. They hired me, and I came up through the ranks.

"It's a decent living if you don't mind moving around. Got used to that in the Army, and nobody shoots at me here." Steven laughed. "The food is good, and people look out for each other. Except, apparently, when they don't." His expression darkened and Owen suspected it was at the thought of someone stealing Drew's body.

From the noise in the center ring, Owen guessed that rehearsals were in full swing. That left the tents empty, which made Owen's job less complicated.

"This is his bunk." Steven stopped at a cot and trunk. "I went through his stuff looking for next-of-kin, but he either didn't have any or didn't want to stay in touch."

Owen looked at the jumble of possessions in the open trunk. People with a traveling show knew how to pack light. The show provided their costumes, bedding, and basic kit. That left just personal clothing and items of sentimental value.

He turned to Steven. "I see ghosts, and sometimes I can get them to answer my questions. It wasn't something I talked about in the Army, for obvious reasons. I'm better at it now than I was then. There's a chance that Drew's spirit is still here, and if he's not too disoriented, he might be able to tell us who took his corpse."

Steven's eyes widened. "You can talk to ghosts? Like a fortune teller?"

Owen winced at the comparison. "Except for real. I work with a branch of the Secret Service where the supernatural is recognized. I'm going to try to talk to Drew, and I need you to keep me from being disturbed and not freak out. If you want to ask questions later, I'll tell you what I can."

Steven stared at him for a moment as if seeing him for the first time, and then he blew out a breath and nodded. "Okay. For old times' sake. But this kind of thing is definitely out of my wheelhouse."

"Thank you," Owen said, relieved. He had been unsure whether Steven would help or throw him out.

Owen spotted a braided leather cord that looked like a bracelet and reached for it, braced for whatever resonance it might possess.

He saw a man in his late twenties with shaggy blond hair and a lost expression.

"Drew?" Owen asked silently.

The ghost startled. *"Who are you? And where am I? Everything's wrong. I was riding—and now I'm here. What's going on?"*

Owen's heart went out to the man. The newly dead were often disoriented and, like Drew, often didn't even realize they had passed.

"You were thrown from your horse and broke your neck. It happened fast. You're dead," Owen said as gently as he could.

"Dead? I can't be dead. I have a show to do. I was supposed to meet a girl in town tonight."

"I'm sorry," Owen told him. *"Do you know what happened to your body?"*

"My body? I thought that was a bad dream. Oh, shit. Am I really dead?"

But even as the ghost reacted in confusion, Owen could see the spirit starting to realize what had happened.

"I thought it was some sort of delirium. I saw myself lying in my bed, but I was standing next to the cot. I couldn't touch my body, and nothing woke me up. I thought maybe I had a fever dream. And then a man came in and picked me up and carried my body out. I tried to follow, and I couldn't," Drew's ghost said.

"Did you recognize who stole your body?"

The ghost nodded. *"Frank. One of the stablehands. I didn't have any beef with him. I don't know why he'd do such a thing. But he came in the middle of the night and then…I was stuck here."*

Owen's heart went out to the ghost. *"Would you like to pass over? I can help."* The ghost couldn't testify and keeping him here would be cruel if Owen could give him peace.

"Can you do that? Please, mister. I want to go to heaven."

Owen couldn't give him any assurances about the afterlife, but he could help him make the passage. He shut his eyes and recited a short incantation, and when he looked again, Drew's ghost was gone.

"What just happened?" Steven stared at Owen as if he had never seen him before.

"What did you see or sense?" Owen couldn't help being curious. Sometimes people who weren't usually sensitive to the supernatural still picked up a glimpse of a ghost or the frisson of energy from a spirit passing nearby.

"I suddenly got cold to the marrow, and I thought I heard Drew's voice, but I couldn't catch what he said." Steven looked shaken. "You talked to him? You're the real deal?"

Owen nodded. "Yes to both. If you've got some whiskey stashed away, you look like you could use a slug."

Steven removed a flask from the inside pocket of his jacket and downed a gulp. He held it out to Owen, who shook his head.

"Just another day at the office for me," Owen said.

"What did...Drew...tell you?" Steven asked.

Owen recounted his conversation with the ghost and his accusation that Frank had taken the body.

Steven thought for a moment. "Frank's new with the show, just hired on here in Chicago. He's a stablehand, so he didn't need to know anything special except how to muck out a stall and not get trampled by the horses. We always hire extra hands when we get to town. They don't usually travel with us unless they have special skills."

"Frank might have applied, knowing that with all the dangerous stunts, it was possible someone would die, or maybe he just happened to know people, and when Drew got killed, he saw a chance to make a quick buck," Owen said. "Let's go find Frank."

Steven put a hand on Owen's arm to stop him from leaving. "Wait. I have questions. You could see ghosts back then?"

Owen knew he meant in the Army when they were close. "Yes, but I couldn't hold the connection as well or hear them as clearly."

"So when we were in battle—"

"It was rough," Owen admitted. "I drank a lot those nights."

"I remember. I just thought it was nerves, like the rest of us." Steven licked his lips nervously. "Did Drew go to heaven? Could you see what happens after?"

Owen shook his head. "No. I'm sorry. I just know that ghosts go on. Where is above my paygrade."

"The Church—"

"Has plenty of theories that don't really work in real life," Owen snapped, sounding sharper than he intended. "I don't do black magic, and most of the incantations came from the Church in the first place. If I didn't lose my chance at the afterlife by shooting men on the battlefield, I don't think having a chat with ghosts will doom me now."

"I hadn't thought of it that way," Steven said. "I guess I thought there would be a lot more fussy stuff."

"Fussy?" Owen raised an eyebrow.

Steven waved his hand in a vague way. "Singing. Dancing. Woo-woo."

Owen snickered. "Definitely no singing and dancing."

They reached the sea of tents that worked as a bunkhouse. Steven asked for Frank, and several of the crew pointed toward a particular location. When they opened the tent flap, the space was completely empty.

"He's gone," Steven said.

"I'm not surprised," Owen replied. "But just in case, you might quiz any other local hires to see if they've got friends in low places who might want to pick up a body on the cheap if there's another death."

He hadn't expected that Frank would be dumb enough to stick around, especially if he had used hex bags or other magic to conceal his crime. Owen thought about asking whether the show had its own witch on staff but decided against it. Steven had seemed shocked by his mention of supernatural abilities, and a witch of any real power should have sensed strange magic being done on the show grounds.

"What now?" Steven asked.

"There's no point in involving the police," Owen said. "I'm pretty sure they're paid off by the local Mob to keep this kind of thing quiet." *And one of the Mob bosses is already looking into missing bodies.*

"If Drew didn't have any family, then there's no one to make inquiries. Pour one out for him and watch your back."

Stephen looked shaken. "You do this sort of thing all the time?"

Owen nodded. "We travel where we're assigned a case, wherever the railroads go."

"We?"

"I have a partner and a valet, who's also a bodyguard. We live in a train car." Owen played down the comforts of his situation on purpose. Steven also moved from place to place, but even with extra considerations for being the head of security, his accommodations were considerably less posh.

"Huh. Who'd have thought, back then." Steven paused. "Look, I can get the night off if you want to meet up in town, have some drinks, catch up."

Owen read the invitation for what it was: commitment-free but certainly not platonic. He shook his head. "Thank you, but I can't. I… have someone."

Steven raised an eyebrow. "I used to be someone."

Owen gave a sad smile. "That was a long time ago, and we're not who we were then. We can be friends, but nothing on the side."

"I'm glad for you, Owen. That sort of thing doesn't always happen for men like us."

"But it proves it's possible," Owen replied.

Steven looked away. "I'm not sure I'm a one-man man. I think I like the rambling life a little too much."

"Just be happy," Owen replied. "And be safe." He pulled a business card from his coat. "We're at Union Station. Look for the Pullman car on the sidelines or send a messenger. Or a telegram."

Steven stared at the card for a moment before pocketing it. "Take care of yourself," he told Owen. "Sounds like you might make some powerful enemies. Be careful."

"I always am." They shook hands, then Owen pulled him in for a tight hug.

"If anything weird happens or you think you're in danger, I'll help however I can," Owen assured him.

"Weirder than today? It would have to be pretty damn strange." Steven released him and stepped back. Owen could practically see the man's defenses slipping back into place.

"I guess I need to walk you to the front gate so the boss doesn't have a stroke," Steven said.

They didn't say much as they headed for the entrance.

"Good luck with the show," Owen said as they reached the exit.

"Thanks. I don't know if you get time off, but it's worth a few hours to see the show if you're interested," Steven replied. Now that they had covered everything, he seemed a little unsure. Owen hadn't wanted to hurt his feelings, but his relationship with Calvin was far too important to risk.

"See you when I see you." Owen tried to lighten the mood.

"Not if I see you first."

Chapter 5
Calvin

What do you know about Settlement Houses?" Abby asked as she and Calvin rode in the hired carriage from the train station into the city. Winston left early in the morning to pick up provisions and connect with some of his contacts in the city. He promised to be back in time to have supper waiting.

"Not much," Calvin admitted. "I got the impression somewhere that they help get homeless people off the streets and give them a fresh start by teaching them skills."

"Sort of. The concept started in England, intending to bring together rich and poor to create a better community for everyone. They aren't just flophouses—they provide lodging, of course, but also classes to teach job skills, practical things like sewing and cooking, plus reading and writing, as well as having a clinic. They're a lifeline to help people get established and rise above their station," Abby added with pride.

"Some of the houses help new immigrants adapt, and others focus on the Black folks who have come up from the South after the war," she told him. "And some are for anyone who needs help. I'll give you a little tour first, and then we'll go see Molly. You can ask all the questions you want."

The first place Abby sent the carriage was a sprawling brick mansion. "This is Hull House," Abby proclaimed. "It's the crown jewel, and the founders of the movement used their connections to establish it. It's known for being well-run, so I doubt your body snatchers are having luck there. As you'll see, most of the other facilities are much more modest, with fewer resources and smaller staff. They're stretched thin, which leaves more room for error."

Abby directed them past three other facilities, which were large, repurposed homes. Calvin saw children playing in the yard and mothers seated in small groups.

"The people who come to the settlement houses are very poor," Abby explained. "Often, they've just come to America and left everything behind. They want to work and do better for themselves, but they need help."

"If they've just emigrated or moved to the city from the South, then they don't have family nearby," Calvin guessed. "No one looking out for them."

Abby shook her head. "Sometimes it works like a chain. One person comes, does well, and sends back for others. Most of the time, people are just trying to get out of a bad spot and find something better. Without organizations like the settlement houses, they get preyed on by criminals or have trouble making ends meet."

The house run by Molly Dawson was a modest two-story brick home with a porch and a small, fenced yard.

"Molly does a good job with her resources. Many people contribute time and money to help. It's just that the need is so great, and there are a lot of lost souls who get here and aren't prepared for the change."

Abby knocked on the door, with Calvin a step behind her.

"Hello, Miss Edwards," a plump woman with graying hair greeted them. "Welcome back."

"Hello, Matilda," Abby replied in a warm tone that told Calvin they were well-acquainted. "We're here to see Miss Dawson. She's expecting me."

"Right this way." Matilda ushered them into a small parlor. The home smelled of baking bread and laundry soap, and despite being home to multiple families, everything was clean and tidy.

They passed through the kitchen to a room that looked like a repurposed closet, which served as Molly's office.

"Abby! It's so good to see you." Molly Dawson was a sturdy woman in her forties with a kind face and silver-streaked brown hair in a bun.

"Thank you for allowing our visit. This is Mr. Calvin Springfield. He's with the Secret Service." Abby dropped her voice on the last sentence.

"Pleased to make your acquaintance, Agent Springfield," Molly replied, as if meeting a federal agent happened every day. "How can I help you?"

"Can we speak privately?" Calvin asked.

Molly closed the door partway and asked someone outside to make sure they weren't disturbed. She sat behind a narrow desk and motioned for Abby and Calvin to take the chairs across from her.

"It's about the missing bodies," Abby told her. "They're trying to figure out who took them and why."

Molly gave Calvin a more assessing once-over. "That brought you all the way from Washington?"

Calvin nodded. "Yes, ma'am. It's part of a larger pattern—and we think there's something very dangerous going on behind the scenes."

"Not being able to give someone a proper burial is sad, but how is it dangerous? I've heard rumors about corpses going to medical schools, where at least they're used to help train doctors and learn about diseases," Molly replied, and Calvin appreciated her practical view.

"We have reason to believe that this is different and worse. We think the people taking the bodies are using them for experiments that I can't talk about but would best be summed up as 'nefarious.'" Calvin hated being vague, but he didn't want word of their suspicions to get out and start a panic. Or worse, get back to the perpetrators to tip their hand.

"Jacob Schwan and his family came to our house a month ago. We treated him for a bad cough. He took a sudden turn for the worse and died in the night," Molly said.

"We do the best we can for people, but many of these folks have been sick or battling a condition for a while without treatment, and they succumb," she added. "I think Jacob was sicker than he let on to get his family shelter."

"Just the cough? No other ailments?" Calvin asked.

She frowned and gave him an odd look. "None we knew about. Of course, there was no autopsy. Our doctor declared him dead, and we put him in the locked shed in the back since it was the middle of the night. In the morning, someone had broken in, and the body was gone. No one saw anything amiss, but then again, we have one night watchman, and he has to make rounds."

"Would anyone have left the grounds after Jacob died?" Calvin asked.

"I wouldn't think so. It was quite late. But it was known that evening that he was likely to die overnight," Molly said. "Why?"

"We believe that the people who are using the bodies for their experiments reach out to workers in places like this and offer them money to let them know about a death," Calvin replied.

"Did any of your workers quit after the body vanished?" Abby asked. "Or perhaps just not show up for their shift?"

"One of our janitors, Peter, called off sick the next day," Molly replied. "I didn't think anything about it at the time. The colder weather has everyone coughing and under the weather. He lived here in the building. But when someone went to check on him, he was gone—and so were all his things."

"Did he mention leaving to anyone?" Calvin asked.

Molly shook her head. "No. And if someone gave him money to watch for a death and steal the body, they must have paid well because the janitor position was one of our better house jobs."

"Do you know anything about Peter?" Abby asked. "That might give us a clue to who might have gotten him involved."

"Assuming that he did take the body," Molly reminded them. "We don't know that for certain. It's circumstantial evidence."

I could bring Owen and see if he can contact Jacob's ghost. But finding Peter without more details will be a dead end, even if we know he took the corpse.

"Do people here know the body was taken?" Calvin asked.

Molly shook her head. "We did our best to keep it quiet. That's such a terrible thing. Our residents have very little besides their dignity. It shouldn't be too much to ask to be treated like a human being."

"What have you heard from the other smaller settlement houses?" Abby asked. "You know everyone who's involved."

"Most of the houses have had a body go missing," Molly said. "Not Hull House, but they have more security, and the police have to pay attention to them. The cops ignore the rest of us, even though what we do makes their job easier by helping people get off the street and out of poverty and crime."

"It's happening elsewhere?" Calvin confirmed.

Molly nodded. "We don't talk about it publicly because how would that look? We depend on the goodwill of the community and the government. But yes, it's happened other places. We're scared. No one knows what to make of it. We can't afford to hire guards. I can deputize more of our residents, but they might not be more honest than Peter was."

Calvin admired Molly's matter-of-fact approach and was impressed that she assessed the situation so calmly.

"Folks are here because they're poor," Molly said. "Even some of our staff started as clients and then pulled themselves together and qualified for a job. Offering what to them seems like a lot of money for something that doesn't hurt anyone would be hard to turn down."

"Given the type of people we believe are behind the experiments, there's a good chance that the body thief won't get paid—but could end up dead," Calvin warned.

"Desperate people are used to taking risks," Molly told him. "Compared to what they may have survived, they might not see it as dangerous."

"When the other houses had bodies vanish, did they also have a worker disappear? It would be helpful to know whether these are all inside jobs or if some involve a break-in," Calvin said. "And if there's a connection between the body being taken and a worker leaving suddenly, it could be helpful to remind the staff of the risks if someone offers them a job that's too good to be true."

Molly took a deep breath. "I can suggest it, but I don't think they'll do more than make a very general statement if that. We're all mortified about what happened and afraid that if word gets out to donors or the newspapers, we'll lose support." Molly paused. "You'll keep what I've told you confidential, won't you?"

"Of course."

Calvin could empathize with the settlement houses' predicament and wagered that whoever was behind the thefts also understood the pressure on them to remain silent and not make a public fuss. Given his experience with police, he doubted any useful investigation would ensue, meaning the houses would have compromised their reputations for nothing.

"Is there anything else I can do for you?" Molly asked.

Calvin shook his head. "No. You've been generous with your time." He took out a card from his vest pocket. "If anything else strange happens, please contact me. Miss Edwards knows how to reach me as well. Thank you for the information."

When the carriage pulled away from the curb, Calvin turned to Abby. "You know her. How do you think that went?"

Abby looked thoughtful. "She was definitely uncomfortable talking about it—not surprising. Worried about the house's reputation. I think she was honest with her answers, and she's scared that harm could come to the residents. Molly's a straight shooter."

Calvin nodded. "That was my impression. She's an impressive lady."

The carriage dropped Abby off at her rooming house, with a promise to talk soon, and then took Calvin back to the Pullman car.

"Oh, good. You're back," Winston greeted him. "I trust your morning went well?"

"Reasonably so. Did I miss anything? Is Owen back yet?"

Winston laughed. "You didn't miss anything, and Owen has not returned yet, but I would expect him fairly soon. But there have been some new developments."

"Like what?"

"I've made contact with Arabella Munson, and she's willing to meet this afternoon for tea at the shop near the train station," Winston replied. "Apparently, the owner is a friend of the coven and will give us a private seating area to talk. It's also warded for protection, which is handy to know."

"Very," Calvin agreed. "Are Owen and I included in the invitation? You've known her for a while."

"Either or both of you," Winston said. "I made sure. And one other thing. Miss Sunderson sent tickets for the two of you to attend the galvanism demonstration tonight with her. I've adjusted dinner time to accommodate the show."

Calvin's eyebrows raised. "The show? Interesting. I wonder if she has a new lead." He checked his watch. "Owen's late." Not enough yet to worry, but Calvin felt on edge.

"Still at the Wild West Show, I presume. He hasn't sent a message that his plans changed."

That meant there was no way to let Owen know about tea with Arabella or the tickets. He hoped Owen returned in time to join them since he badly wanted his partner's perspective on the show.

"Miss Sunderson said she would send a carriage to pick you up. You'll want a bite for lunch before then," Winston advised. "I'll bring out something to the table. Maybe Owen will be back by then."

Winston headed back to the kitchen. Calvin checked the telegraph out of habit, but no new messages had arrived.

Winston returned with a tray of sliced salami and cheese along with a variety of crackers, jams, and spreads, a favorite quick meal when there was a lot going on. Calvin poured himself a cup of hot coffee from the pot Winston brought to the table and reached for a fork.

"Perfect choice, Winston. I'm hoping Owen will get here in time to share it."

"If not, I'll leave it in the ice box for him. But I also hope he can join us."

Owen hadn't returned by the time they were due to meet Arabella, so Calvin left him a note about the food and where they were headed, as well as the show that evening.

The brisk air helped Calvin shake off his post-lunch drowsiness. He and Winston stayed alert, but they didn't sense that anyone was following them. Calvin also suspected that Winston's magic made them slippery to a pursuer who did not possess equal arcane skills.

The tea shop had a Bohemian feel. Tapestries and printed fabric swags adorned the walls, along with beaded lampshades that suggested exotic locations. The unusual décor distracted the eye from real magical sigils Calvin spotted inscribed on the walls.

"We're looking for Arabella," Winston told the woman who greeted them.

"Right this way. She's expecting you."

Calvin noted that the woman's accent sounded Eastern European, perhaps Romani. Even without activating his touch magic, the tearoom gave him a sense of well-protected safety.

"Winston. So good to see you. And who might this be?"

"Calvin Springfield," Calvin introduced himself with a hint of a bow.

"Interesting." Arabella did not clarify what about Calvin she found intriguing. He wondered whether she was psychic as well as being a witch and if so, what she could read from him. "Please come in. We won't be disturbed."

Arabella had long, dark hair worn loose around her shoulders with brown eyes. Her deep plum gown accentuated her striking features. She led them to a table that looked like one used for tarot readings and motioned for them to sit.

"What brings you to Chicago?" She addressed her question to Winston.

"Missing bodies that aren't going to medical schools," Winston replied.

"We think someone intends to sell to those willing to pay for replacement parts," Calvin added.

Her eyebrows rose. "Interesting. And how would that work?"

"We're not entirely sure, but we think it's a combination of science and magic," Calvin replied, not put off by her skeptical tone.

"You know the area covens—both the independent ones and the ones that are part of the Mob Families," Winston put in. "Has there been any recent interest in necromancy or grave magic?"

Arabella whispered a word of power under her breath in protection. "Those are dark magics. No reputable coven would traffic in them."

"What about the disreputable ones?" Calvin asked. "There's always someone willing to use whatever power they've got to make money."

"You sure you want to know? Knowledge is dangerous," she warned.

Calvin shrugged. "It goes with the job. And if our hunch is right and there's money to be made, how long will it be before they start shopping for bodies with particular attributes? No one will be safe."

"You make a compelling case," Arabella said. "I don't think any witches involved are part of covens. There are plenty of lone practitioners who don't play well with others. The covens tend to ignore them until there's a problem, and then it all gets complicated."

Calvin didn't want to ponder what witch wars might involve.

"I don't know any names. This is serious enough I might be tempted to share if I did," Arabella said. "But I have heard some general gossip that might be related."

She pushed a strand of dark hair behind her ear. "There have been inquiries about sources of elemental power—in particular, the Vril and Zodiac Force. Serious practitioners don't take those fads seriously, but they seem irresistible to non-witches who want to be something they aren't."

"I'm not familiar with either of those," Calvin said.

"I must admit, neither am I," Winston admitted.

"The Vril comes from an awful book by Bulwar-Lytton," Arabella said, distaste clear in her voice. "Those who believe in it say it's a mysterious energy source, but they can't tell you any more about where it comes from, and they're fairly unclear about how to harness and use it."

"Sounds like chasing fool's gold," Calvin observed.

"Very much. So is Zodiac Force, which takes the astrological signs and concocts a theory that someone could learn to manipulate all of the occult elements associated with a Zodiac sign and use them like a tool. Utter rubbish, but it keeps the dabblers intrigued." Her lip curled in disdain. Winston's expression wasn't quite as easily read, but Calvin had the impression that he shared her sentiments.

"If those are bogus, then what's real?"

"Necromancy and grave magic are discouraged because the power is enormous, but so is the temptation," Arabella said. "Both tend to corrupt the practitioner beyond the usual dangers of magic. I've always suspected it's because they deal with harnessing souls and forcing them to do the bidding of the witch."

"It's been said that absolute power corrupts absolutely," Winston observed. "That would seem to apply."

Arabella nodded. "We are witches, not gods. Our powers are meant to protect, help, and heal. Not to make ourselves overlords or corrupt the natural order of the world. And yet, there are always those who do not heed the warnings. They eventually fail, but usually after they have caused dangerous havoc."

"Have there also been inquiries about reanimation and necromancy?" Calvin pressed.

Arabella frowned. "Not to my coven. We would not answer. As for the other groups, I can't say for sure. It's been done quietly if someone is asking around. My suspicion is that whoever might be behind this situation is either a witch of some power or has a person with powers as a partner. Usually, they are deluded about their strength and ability to control whatever they raise."

"Hypothetically, if someone were able to harness enough energy—

from electricity or some other source—to reanimate a body part from a corpse so it could be transplanted to a living person, would it require a powerful witch?" Calvin asked.

Arabella thought for a moment. "It's not always the power behind a spell that requires skill; it's the nuance of wielding it. Brute force will open a door or blow up a barn, but for something like what you're talking about, it's the magical equivalency of surgery. There aren't a lot of witches capable of doing that, assuming that whoever is stealing the bodies understands how to gauge a magic user's competency."

The idea of an *incompetent* necromancer made Calvin shiver.

"Does it suggest anyone in particular?" he asked.

She gave a knowing smile. "We are a tight-knit community. Accusations like that can't be made lightly. I will make inquiries and look into it in my own way. If I find something suitable for your agency to handle, I'll let you know. Otherwise, depending on what I find, we will deal with this as an internal matter."

Translation: She doesn't think the Supernatural Secret Service or Winston, Owen, and I can handle this. Maybe she's right. I don't mind handing off something to someone better suited, as long as the problem is taken care of—and the perpetrator is dealt with.

"I can respect that," Calvin said. "At the end of the day, I just want an end to the problem—both the body snatching and the reanimated parts."

"That would be best for everyone," Arabella agreed. "Let me see what I find out. I'll reach out to Winston when I know more. But please—do not meddle with the covens. Many of our people are very private. I can't protect you if you earn their ire."

"OH, GOOD. YOU'RE BACK," Calvin greeted Owen when he returned to the Pullman. "We're having dinner early tonight. Louisa got us tickets to the galvanism demonstration."

"Tonight?" Owen echoed.

"Yeah, just came up this morning after you left. Change clothes if you want, and you can tell me all about the Wild West Show over dinner." Calvin leaned in to give Owen a peck on the cheek.

Dinner felt rushed, but Calvin appreciated Winston's efforts to feed them before the show. Owen didn't seem quite his usual self, and Calvin wasn't sure how to interpret that.

Calvin had decided at the beginning of their relationship, that he would avoid using his psychometry to take information from Owen that he wasn't yet ready to share. Owen had spontaneously promised not to use ghosts to tattle on Calvin unless the situation was dire.

"How did things go today?" Calvin asked after filling Owen in on his meeting with Molly and Arabella.

"Our hunch was right—the body was stolen." Owen didn't look up from his food. "We tracked it to a barn hand who was a local hire. He's missing—and my bet is that he turns up dead. I let their security chief know that it wasn't a random theft, so if they have any more fatalities, they'll be better prepared."

Owen seemed pensive, and Calvin wondered why. "Did everything go okay?"

Owen shrugged. "Yeah—except for how the whole situation is crazy. I was lucky the security chief didn't throw me out on my ear. The manager tried."

Before Calvin could ask more questions, Winston stuck his head into the compartment. "You'd best be going to make it to the show on time," he reminded them.

On the ride, Owen seemed quieter than usual. Calvin took his hand in the darkness, and he could feel Owen relax.

Must have been more involved than he let on. I'm sure he'll tell me when he's ready.

Their hired carriage pulled up in front of the Coliseum, and Calvin spotted Louisa waiting for them. They had all opted for business attire rather than the luxury of fancy clothes for the theater or opera, a dress in muted colors for Louisa instead of an evening gown, and suits for Calvin and Owen instead of tuxedos.

"Thanks for the tickets," Calvin said when they alighted and joined her.

"The opportunity arose and I seized it," Louisa replied. "Decide for yourself whether you think Augustus Gordon could be the mastermind. He's the one doing the show."

The crowd swept them along into the grand showplace. Tiers of seats stretched all around the sides of the huge building, beneath the high arched ceiling. The open center could be used for many things, but tonight, a large stage took up most of the space, illuminated with spotlights.

On the stage were several tables with big silver domes covering whatever they held. A large cylindrical contraption stood at the edge of the stage with wires snaking to each table. Calvin recognized it as a Tesla coil for generating large amounts of electricity.

"You'd think this was the season opening for the symphony," Louisa said. "The seats are full, and there's a definite buzz of excitement."

"How much do you think most of them know about what they're going to see?" Calvin asked.

"A few of them—most likely doctors—have probably heard a lot," Louisa replied. "They want to see proof of concept. As for the rest, some folks just want to be at the center of the new big thing. They're likely to get more than they bargained for."

The next half hour passed as they traded comments about interesting articles in the newspaper and which plays and musicals were coming to the city's theaters. With the seats full all around them, they didn't dare speculate about Gordon or the case.

A blast of music from the small band behind the stage startled Calvin. Augustus Gordon swaggered into the center area to the fanfare, and the crowd began to cheer.

Louisa took a pair of opera glasses from her bag and peered at the showman, then passed them to Calvin and Owen, who took turns getting a close-up view.

Gordon looked to be in his late forties with reddish hair and a full beard. He had a broad face and stocky body and moved more like a pugilist than a surgeon. He turned from one side to the other to acknowledge his fans. He hopped up the few steps to the platform and donned a butcher's apron before he picked up a megaphone to address the crowd.

"Prepare to be astonished, amazed, and disquieted," he boomed. "What you are about to witness is at the very forefront of science. Today, this new technique is groundbreaking and presented for your edification and entertainment. But very soon, galvanism will no longer be the stuff of traveling shows. It will play a vital role in hospitals in every land, restoring and replacing what has been lost."

"This coil generates electricity which will follow these wires into my test subjects, and you will see for yourself the possibilities!"

Gordon removed the dome over one area of the table. On it sat a slab of beef.

"Ordinary meat, like anyone could buy at the butcher shop. Nothing special about it, clearly no longer roaming the pasture," he added, which got a laugh from the audience.

Gordon attached three electrodes to the meat with long wires trailing back to the coil and moved to flip the massive switch.

"And yet, with the application of electricity, behold!"

The coil sparked a brilliant blue, the air crackled with power that raised the hair on the back of Calvin's neck, and the piece of beef began to twitch and lurch like a living thing.

"Oh my God," Louisa murmured under her breath. Owen paled, and Calvin felt a tightness in the pit of his stomach. From the gasps and other noises around them, some of the crowd had similar reactions.

"What makes your muscles move? How can you lift your arm or swing your leg?" Gordon continued. "Our brains send small pulses of electricity through our bodies for every movement. This is completely natural. Nature tends toward life. *Death* is against nature, and I believe that as these principles are better understood, we may finally, one day, triumph over death itself!"

He whisked the next dome away to show a plucked turkey that looked like it came straight from the poulterer's shop.

"Take a good look—this turkey is just like what you buy at the market. It's fresh, but clearly not alive as it is missing both its head and its insides."

The crowd chuckled nervously. Calvin scanned faces when it was his turn to hold the opera glasses and saw a mixture of apprehension and excitement.

"Electricity will not make up for what the bird lacks," Gordon said. "But science can animate the body that remains."

He attached the wires once more, and the blue glow lit up the arena.

The turkey began to jerk and wobble. Naked wings made feeble flapping movements.

People shrieked and screamed. Some of the women swayed in their seats and collapsed onto their companions, fainting dead away.

Louisa's attention remained fixed on Gordon with a grim expression on her face. Owen's eyebrows drew together like thunderclouds, and he looked more angry than transfixed.

Calvin felt a strange mix of emotions, a tangle of awe for the science and apprehension over how it might be applied and who might control the power.

The blue glow faded, and the bird stilled. Once the murmuring from the crowd subsided, Gordon picked up his megaphone again.

"Ladies and gentlemen, surely you can see the miracle of science that is galvanism. Imagine the possibilities! Think of what this technology, fused with medical knowledge, could unlock. The next wave of inventors will develop tools that can be used to combine electricity and medicine in ways we can hardly even now comprehend!"

"He puts on a good show." Calvin leaned over to murmur in Owen's ear. "I'll give him that."

"For a total crackpot," Owen muttered.

"For my third and final demonstration, I hope to make the possibilities of this wonderous new technology clear. Behold!"

Gordon lifted the third lid, and screams came from alarmed patrons as he unveiled a severed human arm.

"Wonder where he got that," Louisa whispered with a wry look.

Calvin peered closely at the limb through the opera glasses. It was pale but did not appear to be decomposed. Although difficult to see at a distance, the hand looked gnarled from hard work, giving him to suspect it might have been taken from one of the vagrant corpses.

Once again, Gordon attached wires and switched on the coil.

The fingers splayed wide, then clenched convulsively into a fist as the forearm quivered.

He cut the power on and off, repeating the reaction. Somewhere in the audience, a patron threw up.

"For the love of God, stop!" a man shouted.

The power shut off and the hand opened, dead meat once more.

"I realize what I have shown you has shocked some sensibilities," Gordon admitted, having at least the decency to cover the severed limb with a dome once more.

"But think of what this means! Not today and not tomorrow, but very soon, this could change how doctors deal with patients who have lost a hand, a foot, even an arm or leg. Could it be reattached? Reinvigorated? We don't know now, but soon this new frontier will become our reality!"

The audience surged to their feet, giving Gordon a standing ovation. He smiled and bowed, looking gratified and serenely smug.

Calvin, Owen, and Louisa exchanged a potent look, appalled at what Gordon had demonstrated and aghast at the enthusiasm of the crowd.

They don't understand what this really means. For someone to get the spare parts, they have to be harvested from someone else's dead body. They're not asking where the bodies come from.

The band struck up again, signaling the end of the show. Two guards escorted Gordon off the stage and away from the crowd as he bowed and waved in acknowledgment while the audience cheered.

They didn't fight the rush, waiting until the auditorium had largely cleared before they tried to leave. Calvin wondered what the others had made of the demonstration, particularly Owen, whose responses still seemed uncharacteristically muted.

The wait gave Calvin several moments to sit with his own reaction, trying to make sense of it.

If I didn't know what we know, I can understand their excitement. It looks like a miracle. So many people lose fingers, hands, feet, and legs in the mills and mines. Being able to heal or replace them would be the difference between poverty and being able to provide for the family.

But how long before the people providing parts aren't satisfied to make do with whatever happens to be available? What's to keep rich people from ordering their parts to match the rest of their body? What then?

Calvin didn't need to be psychic to predict what would happen— hired assassins killing people who matched a shopping list for wealthy patients in need of replacements.

"I need time to think," Louisa admitted when they reached the street. "Let's have dinner tomorrow and discuss. Assuming any of us can get sleep after seeing that."

Calvin hailed a carriage for Louisa while Owen got one to take them back to the train station. The driver couldn't hear their conversation since he sat outside on a bench, but Owen still seemed unusually reserved.

"What did you think?" Calvin prodded, beginning to worry about his partner. He couldn't shake the sense that something had happened earlier in the day that bothered Owen, something the other man wasn't ready to talk about.

"It was every bit the abomination we expected," Owen replied with an edge to his voice. "Although the audience certainly didn't see it that way."

"If the process actually gets put into practice, I wonder what the Church will make of it," Calvin said. "There are some people who worry that bodies that aren't intact can't rise to meet the call of the Lord."

"Screw that," Owen replied. "What about all the soldiers who were injured doing their duty? Or the workers who got hurt on the job? What kind of God would keep someone from paradise because of that?"

Calvin raised his hands, palm out, in mock surrender. "I don't believe that. I just said that *some people* do."

The ghost of a smile touched Owen's lips but didn't reach his eyes. "Sorry."

"I get the feeling that something happened today, something that's bothering you a lot," Calvin said quietly. "Whatever it is, whenever you feel like talking, I'm here for you. I won't judge. I just want you to be okay."

Owen risked giving Calvin's hand a squeeze in the darkness. "Thank you. I just had a hard day. That's all. I promise."

Calvin believed him but thought he still saw something unresolved in his lover's eyes. "Let's go home. I can think of several ways to take your mind off your worries."

Winston had a tray of shortbread and hot chocolate ready for them when they arrived at the train. He listened silently as Calvin and Owen took turns recapping what they had seen and their impressions.

"We're meeting Louisa for dinner tomorrow night to compare notes once we've had a chance to let our impressions settle," Calvin updated Winston. "Although I can't quite picture the showman we saw tonight being the mastermind behind a resurrectionist scheme."

Owen shook his head. "He wouldn't have to be involved or even know about the scheme. Raising the concept for the audience and breaking down revulsion by dangling possibilities works in the favor of the people who are stealing the bodies."

"Everyone wants to live forever," Calvin said with a sigh. "Desperate people will pay any price and look away to avoid seeing the harm done. I hate to think of a world where some people never have to get old, and other folks become spare parts."

"This all sounds most disturbing," Winston agreed. "Helping a person recover from losing a limb could be a blessing, with proper guidelines. Creating an army of soldiers who never die is something entirely different."

Calvin shuddered. "Yeah, that occurred to me. Not the kind of future I'd like to live in."

He and Owen often played cards before bedtime, but tonight they were both too jittery to focus. They took their leave of Winston early, retiring to their separate cabins to prepare for bed.

Soon, Owen slipped into Calvin's cabin, and Calvin folded him into his arms. "I don't know what's on your mind—and you can tell me when you're ready—but let me make you feel good."

Owen answered with a hungry kiss full of longing and promise. They walked backward toward the bed and fell together, shedding pajamas on the way.

"How do you want it?" Calvin murmured, reaching down to stroke Owen hard.

"Just want to feel you," Owen replied, peppering Calvin's neck with kisses. "Feel you everywhere. Need to know I'm yours."

"Always," Calvin promised. "Never doubt that. I'm not going anywhere without you."

In response, Owen kissed him again, and Calvin picked up an underlying desperation that was new. Something had clearly affected his lover, and while Calvin wanted to know so he could set things right, he knew Owen would tell him in his own time.

Their touches veered between claiming and tender, possessive and gentle. Owen's hands slid across Calvin's chest and down his sides and thighs as if exploring his body for the first time. Calvin chanced a firm but not rough touch, owning and confirming their connection. He added some oil, and they rutted against one another, eager for release.

Calvin made sure that Owen came first. "I've got you," Calvin whispered. "Trust me and let go."

He held Owen as his partner's spend streaked their chests, kissing his face and shoulders before chasing his release moments later. Calvin had brought a wet cloth back with him from the bathroom and wiped them down slowly and reverently before tossing the washcloth to the floor.

"Better?" He folded Owen into his arms. Owen nodded and let out a long breath.

For a while, they lay together in silence. Finally, Owen spoke.

"I ran into someone today...at the Wild West show. Someone I knew out there," Owen said quietly.

"Knew?" Calvin wanted to make sure he understood. "How well?"

Owen gave a rueful chuckle. "Very well in some ways—and not at all in others. He's their head of security. He recognized me."

Calvin stayed still, letting Owen tell the story at his own pace, trying not to let jealousy rise.

"I got the information I needed from him," Owen said. "Then he asked me to join him for dinner. I turned him down." He looked up and met Calvin's eyes. "I don't want anyone but you. I love you."

Calvin stroked his cheek. "Love you too. And I don't like to share. Is this what had you off-kilter all evening?"

Owen shrugged. "I had to sort it all out in my head. It took me a while to figure that out. I think…he reminded me of who I was back then. It wasn't a happy time. I was running away from a lot—my family and what I really wanted. I'd meet someone and sneak away and then hate myself afterward until it all happened again. It took me a while to accept who I am and let go of the guilt."

"That's hard to do," Calvin replied. "Society, the Church—they don't make it easy."

"Fuck them all," Owen said with sudden forcefulness. "I won't let anyone make me deny that ever again. We might have to hide from the people out there, but I won't ever doubt again in here." He took Calvin's hand and pressed the palm against his chest over his heart.

Calvin pressed a tender kiss to Owen's forehead and held him close. "Thank you for trusting me. People from before are bound to cross our paths again. What did you tell him?"

"I said that I had someone special." Owen looked up to meet Calvin's gaze. "And I do."

This time, the kiss was long and lingering, saying what they didn't put into words, sealing a promise.

When they finally broke apart, they were breathless. "Let's get some sleep," Calvin said. "Stay with me tonight."

"I'd like that," Owen replied.

The beds were customized to be larger than in a standard car. Sometimes they shared a bed for the full night, and other times they went back to their own cabins, depending on their mood. Tonight definitely called for staying close.

Calvin and Owen pulled their pajamas back on and settled in, taking comfort in the closeness and the lingering smell of sex and aftershave.

"Dream good things," Calvin whispered and pressed a kiss to Owen's temple. "I'll be right here if you need me."

"You always are," Owen murmured in a sleepy tone as if the day was catching up with him. "That's one of the things I love about you."

Calvin started to answer but realized Owen had already drifted off.

Chapter 6
Owen

Now that you've had a chance to think about it, what did you make of the galvanism demonstration?" Owen asked as he, Louisa, and Calvin awaited their dinner. Owen had slipped the waiter money to ensure they had a quiet table where they could talk without being overheard at a restaurant Louisa chose for its reputation for discretion.

"Nauseating." Louisa cradled her teacup in both hands. "Not exactly how I envisioned progress to look."

"I can't argue with that," Calvin said. "It was definitely... disturbing."

"Gordon is a showman, I'll give him that," Owen said. "Although I'm skeptical that he's really a doctor."

"Actually, that part is true. He's a veterinarian, although he lost his license over some dubious dealings," Louisa remarked. "That doesn't surprise me. But I still doubt that he's the mastermind behind the transplant scheme."

"I agree." Calvin refilled his cup from the teapot on the table. "The people who want to benefit from the parts will also want discretion. Gordon knows how to live large and attract attention. I can't imagine anyone trusting him with their secrets."

"Which means that while we now have a very visceral impression of the core process, we still don't know who is behind the body thieves and offering the procedure." Owen sighed.

"About that." Louisa shot them a crafty smile. "I have an idea of how we might find out more."

"Do tell." Owen enjoyed their teasing rapport. He never worried that Louisa would take his casual flirting seriously knowing that she liked both men and women.

"Have you heard of the First Ward Ball?" At their blank expressions, Louisa's smile grew. "Oh my, you are in for a treat. You know that Chicago runs on grift and graft, right?" They nodded, and she continued.

"It's the most notorious party in the city—and considering Chicago, that's saying a lot. The party is a who's who of the city's politicians, mobsters, madams, shady ladies, and thrill seekers, all of whom line the pockets of two aldermen," Louisa said.

"Even the police captains show up. Every year, the ball manages to scandalize in new and amazing ways. Everyone gets drunk and rowdy, mistakes are made, and new blackmail material is collected," she went on. "And I can get you in."

Owen and Calvin exchanged a look. "We'll be recognized. We've already met several of the local deplorables."

"A little magic can fix that for an evening." Louisa gave a dismissive wave. "Have you gents heard of Pearl Hart?" They shook their heads, and she went on.

"Pearl lives by her own rules. She's been a lot of things, most of them illegal. However, she made a name for herself as a cowboy of sorts. She also has been one of our informants for several years, which has kept her out of jail," Louisa said. "And she loves a good party."

"How—" Calvin asked.

Louisa grinned. "Pearl's something of a celebrity in certain quarters. She's not tame enough for the Wild West show, where the men are men and the women swoon. I suspect Pearl could whup most of those duded-up pretenders with one hand tied behind her back. But

I'm quite sure she would be very happy to attend the First Ward Ball—and report back on what she overhears—if I buy her a ticket."

They paused as the waiter took their order and refreshed their drinks, then returned with a basket of warm bread and fresh butter.

"All well and good, but where do we factor into it?" Calvin asked.

"You would be her escorts," Louisa replied. "Owen has some experience out West we can draw on, and you can just look pretty and stick close," she added with a smirk. "I've seen Pearl work a room and there's no one better. Since even the big crime bosses show up at the ball, it's a perfect way to drop bait in the water and see who bites."

Owen and Calvin exchanged a glance. "Risky if we're recognized," Owen said. "But I agree that it's a rare opportunity to have the most likely suspects all in one place."

"Even if the people behind the transplants aren't at the ball, certainly someone in that group will have heard something," Calvin agreed.

Owen doubted it would be quite that easy, but he nodded in agreement. "It wouldn't be the dodgiest caper we ever pulled."

"Great! Then I'll get in touch with Pearl and make arrangements." Louisa beamed. "I think the three of you will get on great."

"Is this a black-tie event?" Calvin asked.

"There will certainly be plenty of people dressed to the nines. Tuxes wouldn't be amiss. I wouldn't be surprised if Pearl wears one herself—or a Western version, at least. She's not the ball gown sort of girl." Louisa winked. "And you'll want to make sure you've got your guns. Come the wee hours, the party gets very…uninhibited."

"I feel like we're not getting the whole story," Calvin said. "We'll do our best work if we know what's really going on."

Once again, conversation paused for the server, who brought them fresh salads with chicken and hard-boiled egg, more hot bread, and a plate of ginger cookies for dessert.

"The First Ward Ball raises money for the two aldermen by requiring all the businesses that want favors or protection to buy plenty of tickets and underwrite the liquor," Louisa told them. "The party itself is as scandalous as you'd imagine, especially once the booze starts flowing."

"And no one's shut it down?" Owen had trouble believing such open bacchanalia managed to continue.

"Oh, they try," Louisa assured him. "And one of these years, they probably will. But there are also plenty of socialites looking for a walk on the wild side who come early and leave before it gets too out of hand. That's the sweet spot you'll want to hit because once the clothes start coming off, no one is interested in dishing gossip."

Owen shuddered. "Yeah, I think we want to miss that part."

"Pearl's something of a celebrity in certain quarters," Louisa said. "She's managed to stay out of jail—sometimes with our help—but she has a penchant for shortcuts that aren't entirely legal. Plus, she's not the kind of woman most people have ever encountered—and she plays that to her advantage. I guarantee she'll have the Mob bosses practically courting her before the party runs off the rails."

"What's her cover?" Calvin asked.

"She's going as herself, but the story she'll dangle is that a good friend who was a star on the rodeo circuit got hurt in an accident and messed up his foot too badly to ride again. We'll see if someone offers up an alternative—for the right money," Louisa replied.

It could work—if we're not recognized, Owen thought.

"How likely are the Mob witches to be there? Or any witches," Calvin asked. "They'll spot a glamour right away. It's a bit like walking into the lion's den."

"There's always risk," Louisa said dismissively. "But while I trust Pearl to work the room, she doesn't fully understand the case, so she may not recognize important information. I don't really want to bring her into the inner circle on this. She *is* a criminal, after all."

Owen tested his sixth sense, but although he read *caution* he didn't get a feeling of imminent danger.

"How sure are you that she won't double-cross us?" Calvin asked.

"Reasonably," Louisa replied. "I think that's unlikely. For one thing, it behooves her to keep me on her good side. I've helped her sidestep some scrapes with the law because she's been useful, but that stops if she goes rogue. I can't say what she'd do if it came down to you or her, but I don't have the sense that she'll sell you out short of that."

Although there's no way to know for certain, Owen thought. *Then again, we've worked with dicey helpers before. It turned out okay—so far...*

"How do we make contact?" Owen asked.

"Let me get in touch with Pearl, and I'll let you know. The ball isn't until the weekend, so there's time to make arrangements," Louisa replied.

"Anything else?" Calvin asked.

"My friend Ida, the reporter, has an in on a doctor who can repair serious burns and injuries by taking a patch of skin from somewhere else and using it to cover the wound," Louisa told them excitedly. "Usually, they take the skin from the person who needs the repair. But sometimes they use skin from a pig—or a cadaver."

Owen raised an eyebrow. "Is that openly done?"

Louisa shrugged. "I don't think they're shouting that part from the rooftops, but it's not a secret in medical circles. The technique is pretty new and came from Europe. As I understand it, the animal or cadaver grafts are meant to be temporary, but still...there's always the possibility for more."

"I can't believe they haven't had an outcry from the Church," Calvin said.

"Maybe they have. I only just learned about the technique," Louisa replied. "And if they did, it hasn't stopped them. Ida is getting me in as a reporter to watch a procedure. As I understand it, the cadaver skin has to be very recent, but that isn't a far cry from harvesting a foot or a hand—the corpse would have to be fresh and kept preserved."

"And you're thinking it's not a big step to go from transplanting a thyroid or a piece of skin to something like a new arm," Owen summarized.

"Just a matter of scale, don't you think?" Louisa asked.

"I imagine a doctor might quibble with that, but as a layman, it would certainly seem likely." Calvin looked as unsettled as Owen felt at the thought.

"I'll let you know how that goes," Louisa promised. "It's a couple of days from now at the big hospital. I'll also keep my eyes and ears open in case anyone else is observing and ask plenty of questions."

"You think some of the same players might be involved?" Owen asked.

Louisa frowned. "I think the medical community is small and tight-knit. Everyone knows everyone else, even if there are professional rivalries. I also suspect that they love to gossip. Even if someone opposed the idea of transplanting skin, organs, or body parts, it's the kind of thing people talk about."

"To a reporter?" Calvin looked skeptical.

"Maybe, maybe not. But Ida and I agree that most of what we learn is from listening to other people's conversations, even if they aren't talking to us," Louisa said.

Once the bill was paid, they parted company on the sidewalk outside.

"I'll arrange for you and Pearl to meet," Louisa said. "Someplace neutral so you can both size each other up. Of course, there's no guarantee that the ball will be a source of information, but I'd lay bets otherwise. Those folks stay alive and in business by keeping up with everything that goes on in this city, and the kind of people who attend the ball have more reasons than many to be able to survive and bounce back from an attack. I think odds are good that you'll pick up good information. Talk to you soon."

Owen and Calvin watched her walk away. "I guess we need to break out the tuxes," Owen said. "And figure out how many weapons we can carry in case we have to fight our way out if our cover gets blown."

"Never a dull moment," Calvin agreed.

BACK AT THE PULLMAN, Calvin and Owen examined their tuxedos to ensure they were ready for a night on the town.

"I'm still not sure about trusting a glamour to hide us from being recognized," Calvin fretted.

"It's a masked ball," Owen pointed out. "We should be able to get some fancy partial masks that do the trick. No one is going to be expecting to see us there."

Calvin looked skeptical, but before he responded, the telegraph began to click.

"I've got it," Winston called from the study. They joined him moments later, and he looked up from where he had written down the message.

"It's from Louisa. She says Pearl agreed and that she'll meet you at a coffee shop she mentions so that you can arrive together," Winston translated.

"Please let her know we're fine with that," Owen said, and Winston tapped out the reply.

"If I may ask—" Winston began.

"Absolutely. We're going to need your help." Owen recounted the plan they had concocted with Louisa, including the need for a glamour to hide their identities.

"That's going to be a very interesting evening," Winston observed. "Your own tuxedos are too high quality for bodyguards. I will obtain two that are more suitable for this event. I can also devise a spell to hide your true faces. Such things can only last a few hours, but it should be enough to get you in, give you time to mingle, and get away."

"We don't know if there will be witches there, but it seems likely," Calvin said. "Will they see through the glamour?"

Winston looked thoughtful. "A lot depends on how strong the witch is. But in a crowd, the disguise should hold unless the witch focuses their attention on you. Seeing you in passing without that focus should maintain the glamour. Notice that I said 'should.' A very powerful witch might not be fooled."

"Great," Owen muttered.

"In a crowded room, you may well be able to evade detection," Winston said. "Given the nature of the guests, you're probably not going to be the only ones with a need to hide your identity. As long as the glamour isn't highly unusual, it might be overlooked as just another sort of mask."

"And if it doesn't get overlooked?" Calvin asked.

"Then I suggest you carry your usual weapons," Winston deadpanned.

"Let's hope it doesn't come to that." Owen shuddered. "It's not the sort of crowd I want to fight my way out of."

"Louisa said that even the police attend," Calvin pointed out. "I'd prefer not to be found out, but if we are, they may just assume that we're on the take like the rest of them."

"Not something I'm usually happy about, but it could come in handy," Owen agreed.

"LOUISA SENT US." Owen approached the woman who met the description his friend had given them. Pearl Hart was handsome, with a strong jaw and high cheekbones accentuated by a short, boyish haircut only partly camouflaged by a hat.

"I was expecting you." Pearl extended a hand to shake and rose to meet them. By unspoken agreement, no names were exchanged. "She's told me about your discussion." Pearl gestured for them to sit. "I wouldn't normally have an escort for something like that, but I understand the reasons."

Pearl was even more direct and plain-spoken than Louisa and their journalist friends. If she bothered with cosmetics, they were extremely subtle, and her short hair defied convention. She was tall and slender with an athletic body beneath a simple, unadorned dress.

Owen had no difficulty picturing her riding in a rodeo and doubted that she rode sidesaddle. He had heard of women wearing wide split skirts that nodded to propriety while allowing riding astride. While such things were considered scandalous in everyday society, he suspected that Pearl was the sort of woman who didn't hold to rules unless they suited her.

Despite her outlaw reputation, he admired her independence.

"Louisa believes you can work the room." Calvin kept his voice low although no one was near enough to overhear. "Play to their vanity to get them talking more than they should about their new secret projects."

Pearl gave an unladylike snort. "Sadly, it doesn't take much in most cases. If I stand still and look in their direction, they'll think I'm fascinated by their brilliance and go on at length."

Owen snickered. "You're right about that. But they're much more likely to brag and posture to you than to us. We'll be close enough, of course, to hear everything. And while I understand that you're quite capable of taking care of yourself, the attendees are an unsavory sort."

Pearl fixed him with an amused look. "That's my favorite type. Proper folks are stuffy and boring."

"We'll have weapons—"

"So will I."

Calvin nodded. "I didn't think otherwise. I suspect that most of the attendees will, except perhaps for the society gawkers in the high seats who want to feel like they're taking a risk without actually being in danger."

Pearl made a derisive sound. "Posers, the lot of them."

"We can brief you on who to look for and who to avoid," Calvin said. "There may be some people at the ball who could be more useful to chat up than others, who we suspect may know more about the situation and might be tempted to brag to the right person."

"Louisa said you're looking into body snatchers who want to use pieces and parts. I'd heard rumors, but I thought they were just wild stories. She assured me that such things are possible. Imagine that." Pearl shook her head.

"*Theoretically* possible," Owen emphasized. "But it's a dangerous area of experimentation because those pieces have to come from somewhere."

"Makes sense. What's the plan?" Pearl asked as if this were a job of any sort and not infiltrating the Chicago underworld.

"Show up, see what you can find out, make the rounds, and leave before people take all their clothes off," Calvin said.

"Aw, that's no fun," Pearl drawled with a broad wink.

"The event has quite the reputation for debauchery, so we want to be gone by midnight," Owen noted. "After that point, anyone worth talking to will probably be too drunk to give us good information."

"You boys know how to show a girl a good time," she said in a wry tone. "All right. I'm in. Louisa set me up in a respectable boarding house and said she'd take care of getting me something to wear that would fit in. It's not my usual social circle."

Owen sent a silent thanks to Louisa despite knowing that the favor would be expected to be returned at some future date.

"Calvin and I will handle getting a carriage and driver," Owen replied. "We'll pick you up. We're your bodyguards, sticking close enough to overhear. The carriage driver will be one of our people as well. Louisa assures me that the fights don't usually break out before midnight, but we want to avoid attracting attention."

"At a party where everyone goes to be seen? Should be interesting," Pearl remarked.

"There will be much bigger fish vying for the limelight," Calvin said.

"I hope you're right. Okay, boys. I think I've got the plan. I'll get the rest of the details from Louisa and see you the night of the party. Sounds like it'll be a night to remember."

Calvin and Owen hailed a carriage to take them back to the train station and waited until they were underway to compare notes.

"Do you think we can trust her?" Calvin asked. "I didn't have the opportunity to get a read on anything that belonged to her."

"Hell, no," Owen replied. "Not on anything important. But we're paying her to get what we need from the party, and from what Louisa says, Pearl will deliver on the contract. Which is all we need."

The problem with working with informants was that in order to have information worth the pay, they needed to be hip-deep in illegal activities. Pearl wasn't as complicit as some of their contacts—as far as Owen knew—but her reputation for self-preservation told him that trusting her to have their backs might be foolhardy if the circumstances went against them.

We deal with shady types all the time. Whatever happens, we'll figure something out.

ON THE MORNING of the First Ward Ball, Calvin and Owen got a fresh shave and haircut. The event might not involve Chicago's upper crust, but by all accounts, the criminals and mobsters who showed up valued style and flair.

"We don't get to wear the fun stuff," Calvin groused as he and Owen dressed for the ball. "These new tuxedos aren't anything special. I like our regular tuxes better."

"We're supposed to be bodyguards. Hired help. Blending into the background, remember?" Owen elbowed Calvin. "And no matter what you wear, I'll think you're the handsomest man in the room."

"You clean up pretty well yourself."

Their job sometimes required mixing with government officials and powerful people. Calvin and Owen already owned tuxedos that could pass for anything up to a coronation. For tonight, they used formalwear of lesser quality, befitting the station of their personas. Bodyguards needed to look good enough not to embarrass their boss but still be able to fade into the background.

Winston waited for them in the dining room and nodded with approval when they emerged from their cabins. "Nicely done."

Owen was pleased that he had managed to tie his own tie correctly for once.

"Let's get the magic settled, shall we?" Winston beckoned for them to follow him to the table, where he had set out a bowl painted with runes, a chalice, and several small, polished black and red stones.

"I'm using black tourmaline and hematite to protect and conceal," Winston told them. "You'll carry those in a pocket. Nothing for anyone to notice, just pretty rocks. The potion is a bit more complicated. I won't bore you with details. You can eat and drink without disturbing the enchantment, although I'd advise against copious alcohol for obvious reasons. As bodyguards, you won't have that option anyhow."

"How does this work?" Owen asked, a little nervous. They had used magic for concealment on other cases, but the ball would need to sustain their ruse for longer than a few minutes.

"The potion doesn't actually change anything. It and the spell that goes with it just set a glamour so that anyone who looks at you sees someone else," Winston explained. "It's designed for the sort of social event where people move from group to group. I don't know that it would hold up for days at a time, but it should be quite reliable for about eight hours."

Owen checked his pocket watch. "That gives us until after midnight."

Winston nodded. "I'd advise being gone before the very end of the spell. No telling how precise the timing might be."

"What about other witches? Will they be able to tell?" Calvin asked.

Winston grimaced. "Hard to say. If they paid attention and suspected something, probably. It's fairly low-energy magic even though it takes some skill to cast, so it shouldn't draw attention to itself—that would defeat the whole purpose, after all."

"People never look at the bodyguards," Owen reminded Calvin. "We're like wallpaper. Or like the serving staff." Calvin didn't look completely convinced, but he didn't argue.

"I hired a carriage for tonight and have a livery uniform, so no one should notice me," Winston said. "And I'll stay as close as I can in case a quick exit is necessary. I have a charm I can wear to make my magic less apparent to anyone who can sense those things, and I'll stay with the servants so no one of power should be nearby."

"I'll also be well-armed," Winston added with a smirk. "Given the disreputable company you'll be keeping."

They each downed a small cup of the potion. It smelled like

seaweed and tasted like spoiled lettuce. Owen managed not to gag and felt vindicated that Calvin also struggled to swallow the mixture.

"I don't feel different," Calvin said.

Owen's stomach gurgled, and the skin on his face tingled like a bracing slap of aftershave at the barber's. "Did it work?"

Winston grinned. "I'm not sure that you'll be able to see your own glamour in the mirror, but look at each other and tell me if it was effective."

"Holy shit!" Calvin glanced at Owen. "You aren't you."

Owen was surprised at the difference. "Neither are you."

The spell's effects were subtle. Hair and eye color remained the same, as well as the basic dimensions of Calvin's face. But just enough changed that while a resemblance remained, he definitely looked like a different person.

"That's just…weird," Owen said.

"Thank you, Winston," Calvin added. "Anything else we should know?"

"Stay away from witches if you possibly can," Winston said. "Avoid mirrors, just in case. And like Cinderella, leave the party before the magic wears off."

THEY PULLED up to the boarding house right on time. The carriage seemed a bit posh for the neighborhood. Pearl waited for them just inside the doorway, transformed from the cowgirl they had met earlier. Her short hair had a sassy wave, and the opera cloak that hid her gown was elegant and understated.

"Thanks for the lift, boys," she said as Calvin stepped out to help her board.

"We'll have someone watching the entrance to the party all night, so they'll be in place to get us out if something goes wrong." Owen omitted mentioning that Winston would be keeping a remote eye by magic.

The Columbian Museum was lit up like Christmas for the ball. The large building had been built as the Palace of Fine Arts for the World's Fair in 1893 and then repurposed to house a collection of anthropology, botany, geology, and zoology, with plenty of room for mingling among the exhibits.

After Calvin and Owen helped Pearl step down to the sidewalk, they fell back like good bodyguards. She held her head high, squared her shoulders, and swanned toward the entrance like she was to the manor born, presenting her ticket and indicating her security detail with aplomb to the doorman, who waved them inside.

Owen breathed a silent sigh of relief to have cleared the first hurdle. As far as he could tell, there was no magical perimeter set and no protective spells in place. That might be folly given the rogues' gallery of partygoers, but it made sense given the likelihood of rival Mob family witches who might be in attendance.

The descriptions of the "palace" didn't prepare Owen for the reality. The party stretched the length and breadth of the ground floor. Above that were the galleries, seating filled with overdressed onlookers. They leaned forward in their seats, eager to watch the riffraff through their opera glasses.

Here we go.

Pearl looked completely comfortable in the rowdy mix that included actors and actresses, madams and prostitutes, gangsters and police captains. Owen was glad Winston had chosen their tuxes, which helped them blend into the background among the servers and other bodyguards.

Guests, on the other hand, tended toward the flamboyant, with silk cummerbunds or waistcoats in vibrant colors for the men, spats, and top hats that were almost certain to be lost or discarded before sunrise.

Any truly respectable women were in the gallery, watching from a safe distance. The main floor belonged to the fancy ladies from the theater or the bordellos, who turned out in bright colors, revealing silk sheaths, feathered boas, and long beaded necklaces. They hung on the arms of their escorts, preening and posing.

Lines were already long at the various bars set up around the perimeter of the room. At one end, on a stage erected for the event, a small orchestra played the most popular tunes. Couples circled the dance floor. Their moves and the nearness of their bodies would have scandalized a regular gathering.

Loud conversation suggested that the early birds to the bar might have started the party before arriving. Owen could see how the ball could very quickly get out of hand, especially given its attendees.

Absent the usual understated police presence to keep the peace at a large event, Owen noted men in black suits around the perimeter, very clearly Mob muscle in place to keep the party from erupting into utter chaos.

Pearl played her role like she was born for the theater. She flirted shamelessly, glided from conversation to conversation, and asked just enough questions to get plenty of answers from men who were already liquored up and looking for admirers.

"—rumor has it that there'll be more of those skyscrapers built this year," one older man told Pearl, imparting the news like a state secret. "Mark my words—real estate is going to be hot next year!"

"—heard they're gonna expand the El, too," his companion chimed in, referring to Chicago's famed elevated railroad. "Can't decide whether that's folly or brilliant, but people are pouring money into it like it'll turn to gold."

Pearl flattered and complimented, making a graceful exit once it was clear that the men had shared their most useful information.

She'd make a great spy. I bet Louisa already knows that.

Calvin's gaze swept the room while Owen's focus stayed close, watching for any immediate threat. Pearl evaded the advances of drunk men without drawing attention to the situation, slipping out of their grasp and retreating between her two guards when necessary to get the point across.

Fortunately, that didn't require drawing a weapon—at least, not yet.

They made a complete circuit of the room in the first hour and slowly worked their way around a second time in the next as groupings changed and new guests appeared. Pearl had a gift for working a crowd, and Owen felt certain that she could have done well in the theater if she hadn't preferred robbing banks.

The party resembled any other, except with guests who were louder and less constrained by the quiet norms of Victorian society. But as the third hour wore on, and the liquor took hold, bawdy dancing and inappropriate clinches on the dance floor became common.

That didn't deter the gallery watchers, who seemed fascinated by the spectacle. Owen wondered if those observers would leave the event before all social order vanished and the bacchanal began. While arrests were rare given how enmeshed the police were with the Chicago crime families, the upper crust still did their best to avoid a whiff of scandal—at least, of the sexual sort, if not financial failings.

"Veer left," Calvin murmured. "The two guys at the table at two o'clock on my right were with Luca Conti at the restaurant."

That didn't guarantee that the toughs would recognize Calvin and Owen, but it could lead to awkward questions if they did, given their new assumed roles.

A tug on Pearl's sleeve and a jerk of Calvin's head changed their direction, and they wove through the crowd sizing up the audience as they went.

"Those bodyguards at the end of the bar," Owen said. "They have their sleeves hitched up. Do you see the stitches?"

Calvin looked that way and caught a glimpse before the men adjusted their jackets. Each of the men had a row of black stitches where it appeared as if a hand had been reattached.

"Guess there are at least two satisfied customers," he replied, quiet enough that only Owen could hear him.

"I know you." The man's voice sounded at Owen's elbow, and he tensed, turning to see one of the men from Barone's restaurant, an older gentleman who had stayed in the background when they met with Luca Conti.

"I believe you're mistaken," Owen said with a cool tone and a fixed smile.

"Oh no. I've seen you before. That little bit of witchery doesn't fool me." His shrewd gaze swept over Owen and Calvin as Pearl continued to talk to her latest mark.

"We're not here to cause trouble," Owen said quietly. "As you can see, we're escorting the lady."

"Either you lied before, or you're lying now," the man persisted. "Which is it?"

"Doing a favor for a friend," Calvin added, not appearing the least frazzled. "Bending the rules for a good cause."

"Whoever cast that spell knew what he was doing," the man added. "Not the cheap cantrip you'd get from a fortune teller. So why are you really here, *agents*. Give me an answer that makes sense, or I let everyone know we've got some feds here." He dropped his voice on the word, but Owen still winced.

"Trying to get to the bottom of some body snatching," Calvin said evenly. "Heard anything?"

Owen saw a glimmer of recognition in the man's eyes, but the set of his jaw suggested he didn't intend to be helpful.

"Incoming," Calvin murmured, spotting the big guy with the stitched wrist and his buddy heading their way. "We've got trouble."

Pearl pulled a revolver from her skirts and fired it at the ceiling.

"Drinks are on me, folks!" she shouted.

The crowd surged, coming between them and the older man. Bodies blocked the two toughs, although they were tall enough to see over the mob, and one of them pointed in their direction.

That wouldn't keep the older man from following them for long, and it would get ugly when people reached the bar and discovered no one had paid their tab.

Owen grabbed Pearl by the wrist as Calvin plowed their way through the crowd, most of whom were either still dancing and oblivious to what was going on—despite the gunshot—or crowding toward the bartenders.

Now I know how a salmon feels swimming upstream.

They shoved and jostled their way through the mayhem, and Owen felt certain that at one point, Pearl deployed a hat pin to clear laggards out of the way.

Once they made it out of the doors and back to the street, Owen breathed in relief before he spotted the two bodyguards still on their tail. He and the others took off running toward where they were to meet Winston. The big men gave chase.

Pearl hitched up her skirts, keeping pace with them as they ran. They didn't have far to go, but the block was nearly deserted at this hour except for the entrance to the social hall as party guests arrived and left.

Owen hadn't expected the toughs to pursue them and wondered what their orders were. *Nothing good. They had to recognize us, which means someone was worried we'd show up.*

The henchmen were closing the gap, and Owen worried that their luck had run out. The sharp clatter of hooves right ahead of them raised his spirits as their carriage shot out of an alley ahead of them with Winston snapping the reins.

He ran the team straight at their pursuers, and a twitch of his hand and magic sent their guns flying.

"Get in!" The carriage barely stopped rolling as they piled inside, and Winston headed for their pursuers, forcing the toughs to scramble not to be run over.

"That was…interesting," Pearl said as the carriage headed away at a fast clip. Owen's ghosts kept watch behind them while Calvin looked out the windows, but no one seemed to be following.

"We've got trouble." Calvin peered out the window on his side. "Two men on horseback, closing fast."

Their carriage sped up, letting them know that Winston saw the threat.

A shot rang out, rocking the carriage as it tore into the top right corner.

"Get down!" Owen dropped from the seat to the floor.

"To hell with that!" Before either man could react, Pearl opened the door, hooking one arm around the curtains to keep from falling out, and opened fire with her free hand.

"Are you insane?" Calvin dove to grab her ankles so she didn't get thrown clear.

Owen opened the door on the other side, using it as cover to fire past the hinges. At this hour, the streets were nearly deserted, but gunshots were bound to attract attention.

Their pursuers fell back and veered off, perhaps not expecting a fight. Once they were sure they were no longer being chased, Pearl and Owen crawled back inside.

"You two are absolutely insane." Calvin directed a glare at Owen, who guessed it was for taking such a crazy risk.

"Worked, didn't it?" Pearl had a triumphant note in her tone. Owen bet it was the most fun either of them had all evening.

"After all that, did we get anything useful?" Owen hadn't always heard Pearl's conversations in detail.

"Replacing amputated limbs isn't normal cocktail party conversation," Pearl remarked. "But I managed to work it in, asking if they had heard of such things and if they were true. They all seemed to have heard the gossip but didn't know more—or claimed not to."

"We know for sure now that at least two of the doctor's 'projects' lived through the procedure," Calvin pointed out. "But who were they working for? And how did they know to recognize us?"

"How about the miracle doctor doing the surgery? What did you hear about him?" Calvin asked Pearl. "I'd think he'd be the toast of the town."

Pearl pursed her lips as she thought. "That got interesting. Everyone mentioned Gordon and his stage show, but when I asked about someone using the ideas in real life, they clammed up. The hemming and hawing told me they knew more, but no one wanted to get into the details. And given the two henchmen and the riders, clearly someone did."

Owen swore under his breath. "I was afraid of that."

Pearl shot him a crafty grin. "Don't worry—I didn't walk away empty-handed. One of the men knew someone who had 'foot surgery,' and it didn't sound like bunions. He seemed impressed, although he said the recovery time was longer than usual."

"If you're getting a whole new foot from a cadaver, I would imagine so," Calvin muttered.

"I couldn't get more details on the process out of him, but someone else chimed in about hoping they could put one of his men's hands right after an accident," Pearl said. "The general buzz was very excited about new treatments and remarkable science but all very hush-hush. I did hear one name—Dr. Jeremiah Humphries."

"Oh?" Calvin and Owen exchanged a glance.

"He's the professor who has an academic presentation on transplantation coming up," Owen said. "Maybe he's involved with more than theory."

"That older man with the crooked nose said Humphries was a miracle worker, but the man he was standing with elbowed him, and he shut up. From the look on his face, I got the feeling he said more than he intended. Trying to flatter a lady gets them every time." She grinned.

"Looks like we'll be going to his presentation," Calvin replied. "Was there anything more?"

"They were talking about someone they knew who died from a bad heart, and I said that maybe someday doctors would be able to replace hearts like parts from a kit," Pearl said. "The old man said he thought it could happen, and sooner than most people think. I suspect he'd already been drinking, and it loosened his tongue. His buddy quickly changed the subject."

"Good work," Calvin said. "We've got a name at least and some corroboration for our suspicions. Anything else?"

Pearl frowned. "I got the impression that the local Mob families have an uneasy peace. Just some of the things that were muttered, the sidelong glares—nothing specific, but there seemed to be tension a little close to the surface."

"The families always vie for position, but sometimes the rivalry heats up more than others," Owen mused. "If one family could lock up this miracle-working doctor, their people could survive injuries with replacements that other groups' soldiers couldn't. That would be a definite advantage."

"Why would the doctor agree to that when he could sell his services to the highest bidder?" Calvin asked.

"It's the Mob. They don't generally give people a lot of choices," Owen remarked.

By the time they reached Pearl's boarding house, they had exhausted their insights into the evening's conversations.

"Thank you," Calvin said as they helped her out of the carriage. Owen made a quick reconnaissance to ensure no one lurked in the shadows.

"That was fun—it's not every day I get to hobnob at a fancy big city party," Pearl replied.

"Are you staying in Chicago for a while?" Calvin asked.

"Haven't decided, but it won't be for too long," Pearl told them. "Places to go, people to see, jobs to handle. Louisa can get ahold of me if you need me. It's been fun, boys. Thanks for the memories."

With that, she headed inside. They waited long enough to make sure no one followed, then Winston headed them back to the train station.

"Was that worth it?" Owen asked.

Calvin shrugged. "I'd say yes. We didn't expect to have the rogue doc handed to us on a platter. Now we have a name. Might be him, might not, but it's a starting point. We know a little more about the local Mob politics and their witches. And Pearl might tell Louisa something she forgot to spill to us, to stay on Louisa's good side."

"Did you mind leaving the party early?" Owen asked, curious about how his somewhat more respectable partner viewed the evening.

"Oh God, no!" Calvin looked horrified. "I've seen a lot undercover since I've been with the Service and infiltrated some real rats' nests. As long as people are adults and participating freely, they can play whatever games they want, but don't involve me."

Owen chuckled. "I thought you might say that."

Calvin shot him a look. "Please tell me you didn't want to stay."

Even at his most unattached, that kind of scene had never attracted Owen. Add in a mix of mobsters, criminals, and witches, and it doused his libido like a cold shower.

"Not my scene. Although the band was pretty good," Owen remarked.

"I'll give you that. Some people had hors d'oeuvres that looked tasty, but we weren't going to get any," Calvin added. "I'm a sucker for those little pastry things. I could eat the whole tray."

"I bet if you asked Winston nicely, he could either whip up a batch for you or order from wherever the party was catered," Owen suggested.

"I think I will. Even if he snickers."

Owen looked out the carriage window. "If the police in Chicago weren't on the take, they could have swooped in and netted a lot of their wanted list just from the guests."

"It was a who's who of Chicago's underworld, plus the movers and shakers who have mutually beneficial arrangements," Calvin observed. "On one hand, it's a travesty to have Aldermen and Mob bosses carrying on like that. I don't care about the minor criminals and shady ladies. Let them have their fun. But it certainly makes clear who has the power in the city."

"Not like that's a secret," Owen pointed out. "And it's not our problem for long."

"Maybe—but if the ability to replace missing body parts catches on in the underworld in Chicago, you can bet it will spread to other cities. Mob families will fight over it, along with other powerful factions," Calvin said. "We've got to stop it here before that can happen."

"Do you think there's a legitimate use for the technique?" Owen asked, feeling pensive after the way the night had gone. "Good people get hurt too. If the bodies are donated willingly and everything is done above board, it could save farmers and factory workers from the bread-line if they get hurt on the job."

"I see where you're going with it, but I can't imagine the Church or other interests supporting it wholesale," Calvin replied. "The priests and ministers are in a stir just letting medical school learn anatomy from corpses. Even when people could benefit, I don't think it would go over well."

Owen sighed. "I suspect you're right. Of course, even if we shut down what's happening here, someone else, somewhere else, will pick up and start over, and only the wealthy and the mobsters will benefit."

"That's above our pay grade," Calvin reminded him. "Let's bust these bastards and get the hell out of town."

The carriage jolted, and Winston rapped on the compartment, three quick, three slow—the signal that they were being followed.

"Shit," Owen muttered. "Looks like they found us again."

"Or someone else was looking for us." Calvin drew his gun. "But this time, stay in the damn carriage. I don't want to scrape you off the pavement."

At this hour, the streets were mostly empty. Owen had spotted a few hired carriages, but even the police vehicles had been few and far between. Too late for most people to be out, too early even for the garbage collectors and delivery drivers, no one but robbers and revelers had cause to be about.

The horse picked up its pace. Calvin and Owen reached for the straps that hung from the ceiling and held on tight to keep from being thrown from their seats.

They had their guns ready, although Owen sincerely hoped they could avoid more gunfire. He and Calvin peered from their windows, trying to glimpse their pursuers.

A featureless black carriage followed them, whose driver had a scarf pulled up and his hat pulled down to shield his face.

"At least they're not on horseback this time," Calvin observed. "We got lucky that we stayed ahead of the last two—they could have tried to crash us."

"But with a carriage, we've got no idea how many are inside," Owen pointed out. "More than two, less than eight?"

"One bright side—if they had magic, they wouldn't be chasing us," Calvin remarked, nearly flying off the bench as Winston took a sharp turn.

"Unless they're herding us." That ominous possibility had occurred to him as they careened through the streets.

The men in the carriage didn't open fire, which made Owen wonder what their pursuers wanted.

Are they in league with the two men who chased us or working separately?

"Maybe," Calvin allowed. "But Winston *has* magic. I'm betting he's already figured something out and is letting them chase us right into his trap."

City streets weren't made for high speeds. Owen didn't lose his seat, but he swore that his hips and ass would never be the same again as he bounced roughly, barely avoiding hitting the ceiling on the worst jolts. One particular lurch sent him hard against the side of the carriage.

That's gonna bruise.

"I think that's St. Michael's Church ahead," Calvin said. "It's one of the most haunted places in Chicago. Owen—summon the spirits. Winston brought us here for you to call in the cavalry."

Even before Calvin spoke, Owen sensed ghostly energy. He opened himself to his abilities, reaching out to ask for help.

"We're being chased by bad men. They want to hurt us. They've killed a lot of people. We're trying to stop the body thieves. Please—help us get away."

The temperature in the carriage dropped. Owen had closed his eyes to concentrate, and in his mind's eye, ghosts gathered around them, moving and twisting like fog.

"Stop the other carriage so we can get away," Owen sent to their spectral protectors.

They saw a flash of light and heard a loud crack and the terrified shrieks of horses. The ghosts swept in like the tide, surrounding the pursuers until Owen couldn't make out the outlines of the carriage behind them, only the shapes of the panicked horses as they broke free from their traces.

The ghosts are angry. They might not have been able to get revenge on whoever killed them, but they'll take it out on the ruffians for good measure.

Winston didn't waste time, urging their team on to full speed. A glance out the back assured Owen that no one followed.

"Tell the ghosts thank you." Calvin still held on for dear life as the carriage hurtled through the night.

Owen sent his thanks and let his connection fade. His heart pounded, and his hands clenched into fists as he held onto his seat. A sheen of sweat covered his back as if he had been part of the ghostly attack.

"Owen? Are you okay?"

Calvin's worry helped to pull Owen from his thoughts. He realized he was shaking with the raw energy of the ghosts' emotions.

"Yeah. I will be." His voice sounded unsteady, even to his own ears.

"What just happened?"

Owen took a few deep breaths to still himself. "I think Winston used magic to break a wheel or two and snap the traces to set the horses loose on the other carriage. Then the ghosts attacked. I didn't intend for them to kill…but I didn't count on how angry they were or how much they needed vengeance. I'm pretty sure whoever was in that carriage didn't survive."

"The people chasing us probably would have killed us if they caught us," Calvin reminded him. "I can't say I'm sorry if that was the choice."

The carriage slowed from its breakneck speed. Owen let go of the strap, but his fingers cramped from the tight grip. He heard the concern in Calvin's voice and appreciated the absolution he offered, but the raw hatred he had felt from the ghosts still made him vibrate with its intensity.

"I know," Owen managed. "But…those ghosts had been waiting to make someone pay for their deaths. I should have been more careful. They could have just as easily turned on us."

"But they didn't," Calvin said in a gentle tone. "You and Winston saved us. Take the win."

It took longer to get back to the station, and Owen guessed Winston had taken a circuitous route to ensure there were no other pursuers.

Calvin and Owen insisted on going with Winston to the stable, given that it was well past midnight. Fortunately, the barn was only a block from the train, but they didn't want to take any chances after tonight's chase. Winston paid the man almost double and apologized for tiring the horses and the damage to the carriage from the bullets. They walked to the Pullman on high alert, guns in hand and Winston primed for magic, but no one tried to stop them.

"That's far too much excitement for one night," Calvin said once the door was locked behind them.

Owen poured brandy for all three of them and motioned for Winston to join them. They all needed for the adrenaline to fade, and Owen suspected it would take more than one shot of alcohol to slow his pounding heart.

"To us." Owen raised his glass in a toast. "One hell of a team."

"To us," Calvin and Winston echoed.

"Quite a memorable end to the evening," Winston said, although his usual jocularity sounded forced.

"That was some fantastic magic and driving," Calvin praised.

"All in a night's work," Winston deflected with a smile.

"Who was following us? The Mob? Which faction? Humphries's people? Someone we don't even know about yet?" Now that the danger was past, Owen felt his anger surge. "Were both sets of pursuers working for the same people, or is there more than one group out to get us?"

"Whoever was in charge sent henchmen, not witches, so that's telling," Calvin mused. "Either they didn't realize we also had some tricks up our sleeves, or they badly underestimated us."

"I'm all for being underestimated." Winston sipped his brandy.

"It definitely has benefits," Owen agreed. "We know about Humphries, but there's nothing to indicate he knows about us. The Contis are, at least in theory, on our side. The Russos don't have a reason to go after us and would probably avoid the risk of angering the Contis. Then again, it could be someone who caught wind that the Secret Service was poking around and wanted to let us know we aren't welcome."

"I don't know if the aftermath will make the newspaper, but I will check when the morning edition comes out." Winston finished his brandy and checked the time.

"We're likely to meet ourselves on our way to breakfast if we don't go to bed soon," he said, managing a tired joke. Winston was usually unflappable, but Owen thought he heard an edge of tiredness in the valet's voice.

Magic takes a toll, and he saved our asses. He's probably exhausted.

"I'm all for that." Calvin caught Owen's eye in agreement that they should all turn in.

"See you in the morning. Sleep well." Winston collected their glasses and took them to the galley.

Calvin turned the lights down and took Owen's hand as they headed to bed. "Are you okay?"

Owen leaned against him, taking comfort in his solid frame and the warmth of his strong arms. "We got back to the train. And for now, we're safe and together. We'll figure it all out in the morning."

Chapter 7
Calvin

Winston greeted them at breakfast with a cheery welcome. "Good morning. Time to shake off the remainders of last night."

Calvin went to the window and looked up and down the platform. "Any sign of trouble?"

Owen looked out the other side. "Nothing here."

"Haven't seen anything strange," Winston confirmed. "Don't borrow trouble. And eat—we have things to do. We're meeting Arabella mid-morning. She's found out more about how the body parts are being managed—and how the transplants are affecting the recipients. And, she's gotten all three of you tickets to see Dr. Humphries's lecture."

"Does Arabella think there's magic involved in the surgery?" Calvin asked.

"Oh, I'm certain there is," Winston said. "The question is—what happens when the spell eventually wears off?"

"I've been wondering that," Owen said. "Reattaching a hand or foot ought to involve connecting it, somehow, to the blood supply and nerves. That's more than surgeons know how to do—at the edge of experimental. Magic could bridge the gap, but if the spell fades or fails, then the part would rot. If that happens, the person dies of sepsis unless magic can fix the infection. It's a risky procedure."

"People who lose a limb might be willing to take the risk if it buys them more time, no matter how little a reprieve that is," Calvin pointed out. "It's like saying to someone, 'You can die now or die in a month.' Most people wouldn't think twice about opting for more time."

"I hadn't thought about it like that, but I can see it that way," Owen agreed.

"It'll be interesting to see what Arabella makes of it," Calvin said. "And find out how dark the magic is that's involved."

THEY MET Arabella at the same tea shop. Her dark blue dress flattered her coloring and brought out her eyes.

"Welcome back. Winston says you have more questions," she greeted as a server brought a pot of tea to one of the back tables where they wouldn't be disturbed.

"We wanted to find out what you've heard from the covens—and we've got a few new questions as well," Owen replied.

They settled into their seats, and Calvin was glad they were far enough away from other tables to speak without being overheard.

"People are nervous," Arabella replied. "We might be witches, but we recognize there are dark powers that pose a danger, no matter how strong our individual magic is. The Mob families are always jockeying for power, and their witches are a big part of that. The rest of us do our best to stay out of their way and mind our own business. Unfortunately, that's getting harder of late."

"How so?" Owen asked.

"Word's gotten around that there might be a new miracle surgery to reattach a missing body part." She wrinkled her nose. "Of course, the gossips miss the part about it not being a piece of the same body."

"What's the word on the street?" Calvin took a sip of his tea, awaiting her answer.

"Mixed. Some people are curious. Others have religious objections —no surprise there," she added. "And there are folks who think it's just a rumor. The stories are all over the place, mostly explaining it badly. If you lost a hand twenty years ago, you're not going to be able to just sew on a new one."

Calvin nodded. "But it seems like doctors do miraculous things all the time these days. What about for someone who was just in a railway accident, for example? If they lost a foot and brought it with them to the surgeon—"

"Maybe in the future, a doctor could fix that, but not now, except for whoever is experimenting," Arabella said. "You'd not only need a good surgeon but a powerful witch. Even then, unless they're reattaching their own limb, the match with a donor might not work. It's dangerous—but desperate people are willing to take risks."

"And not ask too many questions," Owen added.

She nodded. "That, too."

"Suppose someone could cover a burn with a large piece of skin or sew a finger back on. Would they need magic to keep it from rotting?" Calvin asked.

Arabella thought in silence for a moment. "I'm not a doctor. But I've been around midwives and nurses. Infection can set in so easily, and it's usually fatal when it does. Until medicine comes up with something very powerful, it would take magic to forestall rot. Even then, I'm not sure it would last very long."

"Would a spell like that have other effects?" Owen refilled his cup and dropped a sugar cube into the tawny liquid. "And would it open the recipient to being controlled by the witch who placed the spell?"

"Oooh. Good questions." Arabella gave a mischievous smile. "Best I can say is maybe. It's certainly possible for the witch involved to cast a compulsion or at least some sort of control along with the preservation spell. I'm not sure why they'd want to, but it could be done."

"Would the magic affect the person's free will?" Calvin swirled the sugar in his cup before refilling his tea.

"Theoretically, a witch could include just about any order with a deep spell like that," Arabella said. "Tell them to rob a bank or kill their neighbor, I guess. Some people with very strong wills would probably balk and be able to resist. But most mortals are weak-willed. They might consider the crime worth it to regain the use of the body part."

"What about requiring absolute loyalty?" Owen asked. "Reattach the part but demand an oath. It would be a way to build a strike force or security detail of people who will never betray the witch."

Arabella frowned. "Doing it the hard way, don't you think? There are binding spells that can accomplish that without needing to reattach a hand or a foot."

"True," Calvin admitted, although something about the idea wouldn't leave him alone. "What if the witch was a necromancer? The body part was technically dead when it was severed or taken from a corpse. Could a necromancer reanimate it—or somehow blur the boundary between what's dead and living?"

"I don't know," Arabella admitted. "That's not an area of magic where I have a lot of experience, and necromancers are, not surprisingly, rather secretive. Even among witches, there's a stigma. I guess it would be possible for that to happen, but no magic lasts forever."

"Could a person come back for touch-ups?" Owen wondered aloud.

"Touch-ups?" Arabella nearly choked on her tea.

"Would a spell like that be one-and-done, or could a person come back from time to time to renew the magic and keep it working?" Owen explained.

Arabella looked at him with curiosity and amusement. "You've clearly given this a lot of thought. I'm guessing here, but again, the answer is...maybe. Regular witches don't study necromancy. Necromancers don't like sharing their ways, and most witches are uncomfortable with the whole idea. But assuming the basic elements work like other magics, refreshing the spell should keep it working longer— although not forever."

"That would be a way to keep absolute loyalty," Calvin mused. "Toe the line, or the magic fades faster than necessary."

She gave him a sidelong look. "You think like a mobster. Not sure how I feel about that."

Calvin repressed a wince. His rough years with gangs were less structured than the Mob but not that far removed.

"There are stories from New Orleans about Voodoo mambos who have bound reanimated servants with their magic," Owen said. "Surely they can't be the only ones who could do that. A Mob boss would pay a lot to have even small teams of hitmen or retainers who can't be bought."

Arabella shivered. "New Orleans…that magic makes me unsettled. I definitely don't know Voodoo, and I'm not aware of anyone in Chicago who does. I guess a Mob boss could bring someone with expertise up from there. From what I've been told, zombies aren't really raised from the dead. They're living people controlled with powerful drugs and magic."

She looked equally horrified and intrigued at the possibilities. "I'm skeptical about actually bringing someone back to life, no matter what magic is used, even accepting that the…results…would be damaged. But if someone was dying, a necromancer might be able to stretch the time the person has left, and that could include extending the usefulness of any replacement parts."

Calvin and Owen exchanged a look. "Another type of soldier who can't rebel without falling over dead," Owen said. "Perfect for building a small private army."

"Which brings us back to Jeremiah Humphries," Calvin reminded them. "Have your people found out anything more about him?"

Arabella nibbled a cookie and had another sip of her drink before she responded. "He's not a necromancer. That kind of power has a particular vibration. He can do magic, although I'm not sure he's been trained as a witch. There are reasons we go through study and apprenticeships. Magic is dangerous if it's not wielded properly—to the witch and everyone around them."

"Humphries might have a lot of strong natural talent and be self-taught," Owen recapped. "Plenty of chances for things to go wrong with that."

"Yes, and for the spells to be unpredictable," Arabella agreed. "Another reason there are rules that ethical witches follow. Devising complex spells is best left to people with knowledge and experience. Lots of things can go wrong."

"Could he be controlled by a more powerful witch?" Calvin asked.

"Possible, but unlikely," Arabella said. "There are plenty of amulets and protective spells that even a novice can do to shield against that sort of thing. More likely that he's being paid well or blackmailed. If he's gotten on the wrong side of a more powerful witch, his Mob patron might be protecting him in exchange for services. It would guarantee loyalty."

"Maybe we'll get some answers at his lecture," Calvin said. "Convenient that it's mid-day and not evening."

"Professors," Owen said. "If the audience is made up of other academics, they're already on campus."

"I finagled the tickets from someone at the University of Illinois," Arabella answered. "The event isn't open to the general public, especially not reporters. Sounded to me like Humphries wants to be appreciated by his peers to gain status but stay out of the limelight."

"That would make sense if the Mob is bankrolling him," Calvin replied.

"What's our cover?" Owen asked.

"Biology professors from Chicago State University," she replied. "Close enough to make our presence plausible, and I'm banking on with such large schools, the faculty can't all know each other."

"I'm curious to see how Humphries stacks up beside Gordon," Calvin mused. "While he might want professional status, I can't imagine the same impresario approach would go over well with the scholarly crowd."

They chatted about the weather and that day's newspaper headlines as they finished their tea, then took a hired coach to the university for the lecture.

ARABELLA KNEW her way around the campus and navigated the large classroom building to find the lecture hall. She handed off the tickets to the man at the door, who barely glanced their way as they entered.

Three seats in the back row gave them a good view and an easy exit. Calvin glanced around at their fellow audience members. To his eye, they looked like professors and researchers.

"No demonstration table." Owen nudged Calvin in the ribs. "And no generator."

"Any ghosts?"

Owen paused for a moment, then shook his head. "Not yet. And if there are other witches, they've hidden their abilities." Arabella had warned them that she would be cloaking her power during the lecture just in case representatives from other covens were in attendance.

The crowd quieted, and an unremarkable-looking man strode out onto the stage. He looked to be in his fifties, balding, with a paunch. Gold spectacles perched on his nose, and a pipe peeked from a pocket of his tweed jacket. An assistant followed him, a thin man in dark clothing who immediately stepped toward the rear of the stage, clearly intending to stay in the background.

Humphries's gaze swept over the crowd, and Calvin got the impression that the man was assessing the size of his audience. He seemed annoyed that the seats weren't all filled.

Arabella's eyes widened. "The man with him is a necromancer. I can feel the magic. Makes me want to take a bath," she whispered and shuddered.

Humphries stepped to the podium and was greeted with polite applause.

"Greetings. Today, I will share the latest research in transplantation principles, as well as insights into where this emerging medical field might take us and what that future could mean." Humphries spoke like an educator, not a showman, and while his voice was loud and his diction clear, Calvin suspected they were about to be bored to tears.

His prediction was correct. Humphries started with a recap of the thyroid experiments and some work with skin patches for burn victims, most of which Calvin and Owen already knew. Humphries presented the possibility of replacing larger organs someday and the lives that could be saved.

Murmurs stirred when Humphries first brought up the idea of using dead flesh to repair a living body. Two people stalked out in a huff. No one interrupted in righteous anger, but judging from some of the furious expressions Calvin saw in the crowd, the idea did not set well with a number of attendees.

"The crowd seems to be following the ideas so far," Owen murmured, watching the people around them. "Although they aren't all excited about the topic."

Then again, academics are used to sitting through interminable presentations on a regular basis. They're probably half asleep and only here because they're required to attend.

Calvin suspected very few people could make practical use of the information Humphries shared. The academic kept his presentation high-level, never admitting that he had attempted to replace any body parts himself, and spoke in purely theoretical terms.

Humphries droned on, but Calvin noted that the man was long on hypotheticals and short of specifics. He never explained how a transplanted body part might be fully reanimated and made no mention of magic despite the shadowy presence of his witch, who stood in the stage's wings.

"I'll take questions now," Humphries said at the conclusion of his talk.

Hands shot up in the air. He pointed to a man in the front row who stood. "Dr. Humphries, what you've described is difficult to believe, bordering on miraculous. But could you provide more specifics on how the nerves and blood flow would be reconnected?"

Humphries's expression looked like he had caught a whiff of an unpleasant odor. "There are many areas still being studied. You've named a very complicated aspect that is under research. As I said at the beginning, this specialty is in its very early stages."

His non-answer satisfied the man, who took his seat without protesting.

"How do you deal with the potential for infection?" another speaker from the audience asked.

"Strong pharmaceuticals administered before and after the procedure should ward off adverse reactions," Humphries side-stepped.

"What about ethical considerations?" a third questioner asked. "Have religious authorities expressed an opinion?"

Anger colored Humphries's expression before he carefully brought himself under control. "The Church has a poor track record of support for scientific advancement," he said, and muted murmurs suggested the audience largely agreed. "That will be a matter of conscience for individual patients and surgeons."

But the dead don't get a choice.

"Will you be publishing your research?"

Humphries cleared his throat. "This presentation was intended to share leading-edge concepts. I have no plans to publish until we have a larger body of findings."

Interesting. Humphries seems desperate for the respect of his peers, but perhaps he's not keen to have his name publicly connected to the concept. If he's being bankrolled by the Mob, maybe he can't stand the scrutiny. An article like that would make national news—and generate quite a bit of reaction, pro and con, Calvin thought.

"Thank you for attending. This concludes our presentation."

Owen, Arabella, and Calvin moved counter to the crowd, making their way toward the stage and into the wings in search of Humphries.

"Professor Humphries!" Calvin called out.

The witch was farther up the corridor, but Humphries turned toward Calvin and frowned. "You'll have to see me during office hours. The presentation is over."

"You never said where the replacement parts come from, all those hands and feet," Calvin pressed.

For a second, Humphries looked enraged before he regained control. "You don't deserve an answer, but I'll give you one. Donors. Once word of successful surgeries spreads, I have no doubt that many willing donors can be recruited." His icy tone made it clear that he did not care to pursue the topic.

"What if they can't be?" Owen put in. "Are you willing to see the technique fail to gain widespread use over a lack of donors?"

This time, Humphries didn't rein in his anger. "You impudent fool! Can't you see the value? The world can't afford to allow outdated notions to hold back progress. A way forward will be found. Now stop following me before I call security. And leave me alone—if you know what's good for you."

Humphries strode off. The mage, who had been up ahead, conferred quietly with him and shot an assessing look at Calvin, Owen, and Arabella before walking away with Humphries.

"Let's get out of here." Owen plucked at the sleeve of Calvin's jacket. "I think we've gotten all the information we're going to get."

They didn't speak until they were in the coach, heading away from the university.

"What did you make of that?" Owen broke the silence.

"I think Humphries is walking a fine line between his need for people to regard him as a genius and the Mob not wanting him to blab their secrets," Calvin replied in a wry tone.

"I'm not pleased that we attracted the notice of his witch." Arabella frowned. "I'll strengthen the wardings, and I recommend treading carefully until we have more information about the necromancer's ability and how far Humphries's Mob support goes."

"Could you read anything else about the witch?" Calvin asked.

Arabella chewed on her lip. "I'm sure he was shielding just like I was. There were some others in the audience that I also think tamped down on their powers in public as well. I'm sure the witch is a necromancer, but I can't gauge how powerful."

"I'd like to know whether Humphries hired the necromancer, in which case he's in charge, or whether his Mob supporter supplied the witch. In that case, the necromancer isn't automatically his ally. Maybe more of his keeper, with loyalty to the Mob boss."

Calvin hadn't considered the possibility that Humphries and his witch might not fully trust one another. "Do you think Humphries is being coerced or blackmailed into the work?"

Owen shook his head. "He didn't have to do the presentation

today—and the Mob would probably prefer he hadn't. I think he wants to be famous and respected for pioneering a great medical wonder, and he doesn't care who gets hurt."

"Quite the physician," Calvin muttered.

"He isn't treating patients—he teaches biology," Arabella pointed out. "That either means he's an M.D. and doesn't like dealing with sick people, or he lost his license for infractions. Or he's a Ph.D. and not a hands-on medical doctor. Either way, the work he's doing for the Mob is his ticket to fame and reclaiming his reputation."

Their route took them past one of Chicago's many slaughter-houses. Owen shuddered and traded a worried look with Arabella as they approached the large facility.

"Did you feel that?" he asked, and she nodded, looking worried.

"What?" Calvin had a creeping sense of dread but had chalked it up to the gruesome topic.

"Dark magic," Arabella said.

"The necromancer?" Calvin glanced out the window but didn't see the man they had spotted at the event.

"Look!" Owen pointed in horror at a pile of dead cows awaiting butchering that trembled and shuddered. The corpses staggered to their hooves, and their sightless eyes fixed on the carriage.

"What the hell?" the hired driver screeched as the undead creatures lumbered toward them. He brought the carriage to a rough stop, with the horses restless in their traces.

"We can't just sit here." Calvin reached for the handle of the carriage door. "I'm going to drive. You two—stop the cows."

Calvin crawled out of the cabin and climbed to the driver's seat, pushing the terrified man aside.

"Do you see those…those…things?" the driver stuttered.

"Better hang on," Calvin told the man as he seized the reins and snapped them.

"Git up!" The horses took off at a gallop.

As they lurched forward, Owen opened fire from the carriage window, dropping two of the dead cows with shots to the hips, which made them incapable of following.

Arabella's magic exploded the remaining carcasses, messy but effective.

"What is going on?" the coachman shouted, eyes wide and utterly pale. "Those cows are dead."

"They certainly are now." Calvin couldn't spare the attention to comfort the terrified driver since the frightened horses had bolted and sent them careening down the street.

"We're clear," Owen shouted, leaning from the carriage window. "Nothing behind us."

Calvin struggled to bring the team under control. The carriage slewed and skidded, with Calvin pulling with his full strength on the reins as the hired driver hung on, white-knuckled, with his eyes closed, praying under his breath.

When they finally came to a stop, the slaughterhouse was far behind them. None of the dead cows were in sight, and Calvin doubted that the necromancer had tried to follow.

"You're insane!" the hired driver shouted, practically jumping from the drover's seat. "Take the rig and team back yourself. I quit." He ran off down the street.

Arabella and Owen climbed out. They sat in the middle of the street, but for the moment, neither traffic nor pedestrians posed a concern.

"I'll calm the horses." Arabella walked toward the panting team as she murmured a spell under her breath.

Owen remained silent, but his face was upturned, eyes closed, and Calvin guessed that his partner scanned the night around them for magic and malevolent ghosts.

"We're clear," Owen said when he finally looked at Calvin. "I'm not picking up on anything except some local spirits who aren't particularly interested in us."

Arabella stood next to the horses, lightly stroking the neck of the one closest to her. "They're better now. And they know the way back to the stable. I put a light compulsion on them to go there when you're done with them."

"Thank you both," Calvin said. "This is going to be hard to explain once we get there."

Owen shrugged. "We tell them that we were chased by miscreants, and the driver ran away. I imagine they'll be glad to get the horses and rig back safely. They'll just have to get a new person to take us back to the train station."

"Miscreant cows?" Calvin echoed, unable to avoid chuckling despite the situation.

"Clearly from the wrong side of the tracks." Owen kept a straight face as the others laughed, releasing the tension from their near miss.

"First, let's get you home." Calvin turned to Arabella and gestured her to the carriage. "How are you holding up?"

She gave them a smile that was both sad and strong. "I'll be fine. I'm made of stern stuff. How about both of you?"

"Getting chased by dead cows is a first, but we're okay," Owen replied, grateful they were all safe. "Do you need security at your house or a bodyguard?"

"Once I'm inside the wardings, I've got powerful magic and a revolver. No need to worry," she replied confidently.

When they arrived outside Arabella's house, Calvin repeated the offer, and she turned them down again. "Believe me, the wardings are as deadly as any marksman," she told them. "I'll be safe. You're the ones who need to watch your backs."

"Thank you for everything," Owen said. "Be careful. The stakes are big enough that people are likely to play rough if they think someone is trying to shut them down."

She gave a crafty smile. "Let them try."

They waited to make sure she got inside safely, then let the horses take them to their stable. Calvin spun a tale of a close call with a robber and a cowardly driver. When the stable master realized that the only recompense they wanted was for someone to drive them home, he agreed immediately and called for a new coachman and fresh horses.

"What did you make of that?" Calvin asked as they headed back to the train station.

"I think we're narrowing in on the how. What we need now is the who," Owen replied. "And I'd like a better idea of whether Humphries has magic himself and how powerful his witch is before we go in guns blazing."

"Agreed. This was going to be dangerous enough when we were just going after a mad scientist," Calvin said. "The witchy part ups the stakes."

They kept a lookout for anyone following them, but neither man spotted anything suspicious. Owen generously tipped the driver, and they headed into the Pullman car, where Winston greeted them with a letter in hand and a worried expression.

"I expected you earlier. Did you encounter difficulty?" Winston visually searched them for injuries.

"We're safe, but we had an unplanned adventure," Calvin replied. "We promise to tell you all about it. What's that?" He nodded toward the letter.

"This just arrived by messenger. It's addressed to Owen."

Calvin and Owen exchanged a look. "Not many people know we're here," Calvin said. "And the handwriting doesn't look like either Louisa's or Abby's."

Owen's expression shuttered. "It's from Steven—my contact at the Wild West show."

Calvin tried not to react. *Owen told me that he and Steven are long in the past. So why does getting a letter bother me?*

Owen started to open the envelope, and Calvin turned to leave. "Stay," Owen said. "There's nothing he has to say that both of you can't hear."

"Dear Owen," Owen read aloud and winced at the salutation. "I've found out more about the situation we discussed. In particular, what made the helper get involved. Heard some other things you'll want to know as well. Come out to the showgrounds, and the people up front will get me for you. Stay safe, Steven."

"You should go." Calvin wrestled with his feelings. Owen had never given him any reason to doubt his loyalty or his love. Calvin rarely felt more than a passing jealousy about a boyfriend's old flame.

And yet, he felt a real stab of anger and possessiveness that made him blush.

"*We* are going together, or not at all." Owen gave him a look that made Calvin wonder if his partner could read his mind. "I have nothing to say to Steven on a personal level, so if this is some sort of ruse for a second chance, it won't work. And if he does have real information, he can share it with both of us."

Calvin felt ashamed at the relief that flooded through him at Owen's response since he didn't want Owen to think he doubted his faithfulness.

If the situation were reversed and I had run into an old flame, I'd want to reassure Owen that there was nothing going on. I guess I should be glad that I care enough about him to be this jealous.

"It's too late today," Owen said. "We can go in the morning. They start early at the show. It's quite a production."

"I'm still adjusting to the discovery that you weren't a cowboy." Calvin tried to lighten the mood.

"Nope, sorry. Just a soldier. We rounded up crooks, not cows," Owen replied, although from the look in his eyes, Calvin knew his boyfriend hadn't forgotten the issue. "And after tonight, I can do without seeing another cow for a long time."

They went to the parlor and Winston poured a measure of whiskey for each of them, which they accepted gratefully, taking turns telling the story of their dramatic drive back from the seminar.

"I'll be happy to drive the carriage tomorrow to the Wild West show," Winston offered. "I don't have any errands that can't wait, and that might work out for the best, considering what you encountered today."

"I'd appreciate that," Owen said. "I'm reasonably sure we can trust Steven—meaning, this isn't a trap. But...I think it bears caution. Just in case."

Calvin felt chagrined that he had been so focused on Owen's history with Steven that he hadn't considered the possibility of betrayal. He felt a flush of shame and hoped for Owen's sake that Steven was trustworthy.

"We can head out after breakfast," Calvin added. "That leaves plenty of time to follow up on any leads he might have."

"Thank you." Owen met his gaze. "And despite everything, I think you might find the show itself entertaining. The performers are talented, and they do breathtaking stunts. But it's the theatrical version of the West, not the real thing."

Winston made a hearty beef stew with potatoes, rutabagas, warm bread, and sugar cookies for dessert. Afterward, Owen and Calvin settled in on the couch to read, along with a pot of hot chocolate.

Owen made a point of finding reasons to touch Calvin, brushing hands together when he refilled his partner's cup or trailing his fingers gently across Calvin's shoulder when he got up to use the restroom.

"You seem...off," Calvin observed when Owen returned.

Owen gave a moody shrug. "Off-kilter, I guess, about the letter. Wanting to make sure you understand that Steven is long in the past for me. What you and I have is so much more important."

Calvin reached out to take his hand and drew Owen to sit close to him. "I do believe you. And I also can't help feeling a little jealous that he got to know you at a time of your life that I didn't."

Owen barked a harsh laugh. "You didn't miss anything, trust me. I took the job too seriously and the relationships not seriously enough."

Calvin rubbed his thumb over the back of Owen's hand. "I wasn't in a good place back then either. Getting over my wild days. I guess we were lucky to get together at exactly the right time."

They made an early night of it, turning in not long after Winston let them know he was heading to bed. Calvin pulled Owen into his arms when they slipped beneath the covers and pulled him tight.

"What do you need?" He slid his hand up and down Owen's back.

"You. Just you." Owen leaned in to kiss Calvin slow and hungry.

Calvin used his body to let Owen know how much he mattered, pressing kisses down his neck and across his shoulders, tweaking his nipples before slicking his hand and reaching down for Owen's cock.

"Want you to feel good," Calvin murmured, loving how Owen leaned into him. His possessive streak surprised him since he had rarely felt that way about a lover. Then again, most of his liaisons had been quick tumbles, not actual relationships. For a long time, he hadn't considered that such a thing might be possible for someone like him.

Then he had met the two men who owned his favorite Italian restaurant in Boston, Cesare and Angelo. At first, Calvin had assumed they were brothers despite the lack of a strong resemblance. They worked shoulder-to-shoulder in the kitchen, sometimes arguing loudly and singing off-key at other times. What shone through was their affection for one another, whether it came out as teasing or quiet praise.

Calvin had been surprised to learn they were just friends, but he noticed that they shared an apartment above the restaurant, and although well into their middle years, neither man had married. No one thing made him suspect their secret; rather, many small details suddenly fell into place for him watching the two men argue in the kitchen like an old married couple, and then accidentally overhearing Cesare's apology.

They're together. Really together. And they're like me.

Calvin's world had tilted at that revelation. While he had never put much credence in the Church's or society's condemnation for liking other men, he had assumed it meant he would be a lifelong bachelor. The realization that he might find someone to love who loved him back shook him to his foundations and gave him hope.

All of which was why Calvin intended to hold onto the best thing that had ever happened to him and fight to keep his forever partner.

"Less thinking, more touching." Owen flicked his tongue in the hollow beneath Calvin's ear and made him shiver.

Calvin stroked Owen's cock, then wrapped his hand around both their shafts and jerked them off slowly, relishing the friction as they rubbed together. Owen gave himself over to the sensation, eyes closed and head thrown back, holding on to Calvin's shoulders hard enough to leave fingerprints.

They came within seconds of one another. Calvin felt pleased he was responsible for Owen's flushed skin and blown-wide pupils.

"I love you," he murmured, using an undershirt to clean them both up. "Never doubt that."

"I love you too," Owen replied. "And I don't doubt you. Please don't doubt me."

Calvin did his best to reassure Owen with his kiss. Afterward, when Owen had turned to face away, Calvin snuggled up behind him with one arm draped over Owen's shoulder. Owen twined their fingers together.

"Try to get some sleep without worrying about tomorrow." Calvin nuzzled into his neck.

"Can't promise, but I'll do my best," Owen said in a sleepy, fucked-out voice that Calvin loved. Owen fell asleep quickly, but Calvin lay awake for a while, unable to block out thoughts about the case until he finally drifted off after the clock struck midnight.

"Tell me more about this Wild West show," Calvin said as they headed out after breakfast the next day.

"People back East read all these thrilling tales about the West," Owen replied. "It's true that there was danger, wild animals, an unforgiving landscape, harsh weather, and none of the support systems we take for granted. Not to mention that there were people already living on the land who had been there for generations and weren't keen to have it taken away. Can't say I blame them."

Owen paused, and Calvin figured he was gathering his memories. "The newspapers sensationalized things, of course. Sold more copies that way. The truth was it was lonely, dangerous work. The weather could be freezing cold or baking hot, and the wind on the prairie never stopped," Owen recalled.

"If you were from a settled area, it seemed like a whole lot of nothing out there. No police, no fire departments, none of the things city people take for granted. Sometimes it was hard to find water. Other than some basic supplies, what you could hunt is what you had for dinner. Didn't catch anything? You went hungry. And that's on top of days spent on horseback or jostling around in the back of a wagon. If you were lucky, there was a trail, but it was nothing like the roads back East.

"It was the promise of a fresh start that kept everyone going, and that was the romance of the West that the newspaper stories sold. All of the inconveniences and dangers were turned into thrilling adventures. They left out the part where a lot of people died," Owen said.

He was quiet for a moment and then started to talk again. "A guy named Buffalo Bill Cody is the most famous Wild West showrunner, but there are dozens of other performances, and they travel all over the East," Owen said. "Real cowboys demonstrate roping and riding and do tricks on horseback. Then there's sharpshooting, knife throwing, and archery. They pay the native people to do their dances and sing. Sometimes they stage a mock battle or do a big parade. All very exciting."

Calvin angled his head to look at Owen. Something in the other man's voice suggested that the excitement of the spectacle was hollow.

"If you didn't know how it really was, it's a grand exhibition," Owen said. "But they only show the good parts. Folks died of all kinds of things that aren't as common in the settled areas—dysentery, cholera, measles. People got hurt and wounds went bad. There were a few doctors but not many hospitals. Travelers froze to death in blizzards. Most settlers didn't know what they signed up for until it was too late to turn back."

Calvin figured that while Owen hadn't been a cowboy, his time in the Army had given him a front-row seat to the tribulations he described.

"Sometimes the Army had to step in if the settlers got sideways with the native people over land or got themselves in a jam with a flood or a snowstorm," Owen continued. "Once they did pick a place to settle, they had to build everything from scratch. It was a hard go until they finally had a town and could get crops in the fields and herds onto the range. But that's not what the Wild West show is about."

"I get it, I think," Calvin admitted. "All those things sound exciting until you realize how hard, dangerous, and uncomfortable it must have been. And I'll be the first to watch a marksman or an archery competition. As for everything else, it's like going to the theater on a grand scale."

"With horses."

"That, too," Calvin agreed. "How do you think Steven ended up with the show?"

Owen was quiet for a moment. "I imagine he got tired of the Army and wanted something that gave him freedom and still paid the bills. He uses his military background as head of security. Gives him a sense of authority. He gets to move around and see new places without the risk. Not a bad gig if you don't want to settle down."

Sounds like what we do, only without the magic and monsters.

WHEN THEY ARRIVED at the Wild West show, Owen checked in with the guard at the gate, who glanced at a roster and let them through once Owen vouched for Calvin.

Calvin had been curious about Steven, looking for an insight into what sort of man Owen had been attracted to—however briefly—before their relationship. To his surprise, Steven was close to Owen's height, stocky, with hair a darker shade of blond and green eyes. Nothing at all like Calvin's dark hair and blue eyes, or his height and build. He wasn't sure what to make of that or if it meant anything, considering how varied his former partners had been.

"Owen. Thank you for coming out." Steven greeted him with a handshake that gave no indication of more than a professional relationship.

"Of course. Steven, this is my partner, Calvin Springfield. Calvin, this is Steven Coleridge."

Calvin picked up a slight hesitation before Steven shook his hand. He felt the man's gaze rake over him, sizing him up, perhaps with the same questions Calvin had harbored about Owen's choices.

"Partner?" Steven glanced at Owen as he released Calvin's hand.

"*Partner.* We're both Secret Service," Owen confirmed. Calvin noticed that he left off the supernatural part of their agency name. Although if Steven had called about something to do with their case, he must at least have had an inkling that they investigated situations that were out of the ordinary.

Steven nodded and gave Calvin the once-over again. "Nice to meet you. I hope you can help because I didn't know who else to call."

"What's going on?" Owen asked, all business as he and Calvin fell into step beside Steven as they walked.

"You said to contact you if I thought anything strange was happening. I might be wrong, but I think someone is sabotaging the show, maybe even targeting certain performers for injuries," Steven told them after he glanced around to make sure no one else was nearby.

"Our people are professionals, and they are very careful. They know that cutting corners could cost lives," he went on. "We don't have anyone new in jobs that worked closely with the people who had accidents. I hate to say it, but if my suspicions are right, we've been sold out by one of our own."

"Do you have any rival shows that might have sent a saboteur?" Calvin asked. Chicago had plenty of traveling shows of all sorts. While he doubted there was another cowboy-themed event, every form of entertainment technically competed with all the others.

Steven shrugged. "I guess it's possible but unlikely. Our gate guards patrol all day and night. Mostly fending off horse thieves, but also to keep out daredevils."

"What's been going on?" Owen looked tense, and Calvin suspected he worried that there might be friction.

"Bridles cut, saddle straps weakened, some of the wooden jumping barriers tampered with," Steven replied. "That's not a prank. Our riders put their lives on the line with their stunts. Having their gear fail will get them badly injured—or dead."

Calvin respected the man's concern for the entertainers. "How about the horses? Has anyone bothered them?"

"No, thank heavens. We have stablehands who take turns sleeping in the barns, and horses are hard to sneak up on," Steven replied.

"No one else has died?" Owen asked.

"No. But if the accidents keep happening, something will go wrong sooner or later." Steven sounded like he wanted to take on whoever had caused the damage and mete out his own rough justice. Calvin couldn't blame him.

Despite himself, Calvin liked Steven. He grudgingly admitted that he could see what had initially attracted Owen, even if Steven wasn't the settling-down type.

"I'm not a secret agent," Steven joked, "but I can be nosy. I asked around about the worker who stole the body. Sounds like he owed money, and he might have been on the run from the law. Some of the guys thought he was being blackmailed."

He sighed. "That wouldn't be the first time someone came to the show for a fresh start or to hide from the police. Not all our folks, but there are a few who like moving around because they have something —or someone—chasing them."

"We make it clear that whatever baggage a new hire has can't interfere with the show or threaten the safety of the other performers," Steven continued. "Most of the time, that works. We've turned a blind eye more than once if debt collectors or jealous boyfriends came looking. But the show is serious business. We don't knowingly hire criminals."

"No one saw anything unusual when the vandalism occurred?" Owen pressed.

"No. Once the gates close for the night, there shouldn't be anyone here who isn't on the payroll," Steven replied. "For as big as the show seems, our crew is fairly small and pretty tight. Someone sneaking around after hours should be easy to spot."

Unless they used magic to cloak themselves, Calvin thought. He traded a glance with Owen that let him know his partner had the same thought.

"Do you know who was blackmailing the worker to steal the body?" Calvin asked. "That might give us a new angle to investigate."

"Someone in the Mob. Not surprising since this is Chicago," Steven replied.

"Do you know why he was being blackmailed?" Owen asked.

"Does it matter?"

Owen shrugged. "It might. Leads turn up in surprising places."

Steven frowned. "No one I talked to seemed to know for certain. Not surprisingly, it wasn't something he'd talked about. But the best guess was that he had been a fence for other thieves. The gossip said that his gang had gotten sideways with the Mob for not paying their dues. Another version says they stole from someone under Mob protection. A bad bargain, either way."

Calvin remembered Luca Conti, the mobster whose people seemed to know too much about the missing bodies and the *strega* who had been prominent at their meeting. He felt sure that Owen's thoughts went in the same direction.

"Why would the body thief stick around Chicago with the show instead of hopping a train out of town?" Owen asked.

"Maybe someone promised him that doing a job for them would put him back in the Mob's good graces," Calvin said. "Obviously, they lied."

"Or there are different players who are at odds with each other," Owen proposed. "Because if the body thief was already with the show and they wanted to sabotage the acts, he'd be valuable. Why kill him off?"

Calvin's mind raced as he tried to put the pieces together. "They might have thought he was compromised and didn't want him getting arrested and spilling what he knew to the cops. Or they might not have planned to cause more deaths when they took advantage of the accident."

Steven looked from Calvin to Owen, trying to figure out their conversation. "Please tell me you don't believe the stories about the mad doctor."

Both Calvin and Owen turned to look at him. "Mad doctor?" Owen asked.

Steven licked his lips and glanced around again to make sure no one was close enough to hear. "It's just loose talk, the kind that goes around the barracks when men have time on their hands. But there's a rumor that either a witch or a mad doctor is stealing bodies to bring them back to life.

"We heard a lot of talk like that near New Orleans, about Voodoo and dark magic," Steven went on. "It really spooked the crew, and I think they were happy to head north after that. But up here, everyone's chasing the latest new invention and scientific breakthrough. A mad doctor reviving the dead fits right in."

Their pause made Steven look from Calvin to Owen. "Oh, no. That stuff isn't real, is it?"

Owen sighed, and Calvin guessed his partner hadn't wanted to explain too much to Steven, although that now seemed unavoidable.

"Not exactly," Owen said. "Have you heard about the galvanism displays? The quack who is making sides of beef twitch with electricity?"

"Yes." Steven paled. "I'm hoping that's not tied up in this somehow."

"We believe it is," Calvin said. "Along with a fair bit of dark magic."

"I can accept being able to see ghosts, but magic? That's just in fairy tales." Steven looked perplexed when he searched their faces and found they were serious.

"Real magic isn't like in the penny dreadfuls," Owen replied. "There are a lot of reasons witches keep their abilities hidden. But magic, combined with galvanism, might enable an unscrupulous doctor to use a body part from a fresh corpse and reattach it to a living person—at least for a while."

Steven reached for a flask in his back pocket and took a swig. "I wish I thought you were kidding."

"We're not," Calvin replied. "We're actually part of a branch of the Secret Service that deals with the supernatural. That's what brought us to Chicago. Because if someone is mixing medicine and magic, it's not the godsend it might appear to be. There are a lot of ways for it to go very wrong. Not to mention being illegal."

"The witch would likely gain a fair amount of control over the person getting the replacement part in order to sustain the magic. That could be bad in a lot of ways," Owen picked up. "It's back-alley stuff, unregulated, no rules. And while it's awful enough to steal pieces from dead bodies, there's the potential for someone to 'custom order' a part to better match the host body."

"Rather than taking a chance on a homeless person who might not be healthy, getting a body part from an athlete could be attractive," Calvin added.

"You're serious."

"We came to Chicago to track down rumors, and if there is a mad doctor, we're here to shut him down," Owen said.

Calvin could practically see the wheels turning in Steven's head as he wrestled with the unfamiliar ideas and then had them fall into place.

"Okay. I guess you learn something new every day, huh? I don't understand everything, but I want to protect my people. What can I do to help?"

A glimmer of pride flickered in Owen's eyes, and Calvin's liking of the security chief increased. "Keep your eyes and ears open," Owen replied. "And contact us if you get a lead. The folks we think are behind this are dangerous—Mob and witches—so don't try to go up against them on your own. That's why the feds got sent in—us."

"What now?" Steven asked. "My job is to keep the people here safe. I don't want them getting killed to be replacement parts."

Calvin weighed the options. A public venue like the rodeo was difficult to secure with spells because so many strangers needed to come and go. Protective charms might help, but they were unlikely to hold up against a powerful witch and only worked if the owner of the talisman kept it constantly on their person.

"Stay alert, and let us know if you see anything suspicious," Owen replied. "We're working this from a couple of angles. Once we pull the pieces together, we're here to shut it down."

"I just want to keep my crew safe," Steven said. "I'll help any way that I can. And—thank you for taking me seriously. I can't tell the show management. They'd think I'd been drinking and laugh me out of their office."

Skepticism and downright denial about the occult always made the job of protecting civilians more difficult.

"You know how to reach us," Owen said. "Keep your eyes open and your wits about you, and stay safe."

"You, too," Steven said. "Although now that I know the woo-woo is real, I might never sleep well again."

Chapter 8
Owen

Dabblers forget—magic always leaves a signature." Arabella looked smug as she lifted her cup of hot chocolate and took a sip. A few days had passed, and she seemed none the worse for their recent adventure.

"You've found where Humphries is doing his surgery?" Calvin reached for a cookie. The bakery where they had agreed to meet had caught his eye a few days ago, and their goods were as tasty as they looked.

"We need to be sure," Owen pressed.

Arabella fixed him with a look. "We're sure. We've been keeping watch. Humphries and some others go in and out. Once in a while, a delivery carriage big enough to hold a body—or a coffin—pulls up and unloads. The sign says it's a leather workshop, but no customers or employees ever come around. It's in a shady neighborhood. And it reeks of dark magic."

"I can attest to that firsthand," Winston vouched. "Just driving by made me nauseous. I don't think anyone with even a glimmer of power could stand to be anywhere near the location for long."

Owen's magic also picked up on the truth in Arabella's report. "What about your coven? Will they help?"

"Yes. Humphries isn't one of ours, and what he's doing feeds the kind of fear that leads to witch hunts. He's a threat to us all. Not to mention that the use of magic for his purposes is utterly abhorrent."

"What kind of protections does his surgery location have? What about guards?" Calvin asked.

"If he has security, they're inside. The magic deflects attention and the building has been glamoured to appear uninteresting, even ramshackle," Arabella reported.

"I don't doubt there are guards inside. Perhaps even some of the beneficiaries of the replacement parts. I would expect them to be co-opted in return for being repaired," Winston added with distaste.

"Do they live there? If not, they have to come and go," Calvin said.

"If it's too dangerous to have someone watch the location, I can ask the ghosts," Owen volunteered. "I should be able to contact them without tripping any alarms about using magic."

"Someone has to be funding Humphries," Calvin fretted. "The question is—who?"

"That's a question for Louisa." Owen knew that their Pinkerton friend could get the financial information. "It would be good to know who has a stake in the game. Because Humphries has to have a benefactor."

"It's likely to be one of the Mob families, although Luca Conti looked genuinely surprised," Calvin said. "If one family gained the ability to put their disabled strongmen back on the job, it would be an advantage."

"Sounds expensive—I'd think burly henchmen would be a dime a dozen," Winston sniffed.

"Think about it—the Mob values absolute loyalty. That cuts both ways," Owen said. "If they take good care of their people, those folks are completely trustworthy—and having magic involved in keeping the replacement part would also help."

"Extreme, but I can see that," Calvin admitted.

"The Mob covens keep to themselves," Arabella said. "They're secretive, even for witches. But I may have some contacts who can find out enough to narrow it down."

"What about the Russo family? They're vying with the Contis for the upper hand." Calvin took another long sip and paused to savor the drink before setting down his cup.

"They've been the most visible, but that doesn't always mean something. The real power could be staying out of the limelight," Winston pointed out.

"I'll see what I can find out," Arabella promised. "What's the plan?"

Calvin and Owen exchanged a glance. "I'd like to see where Humphries has set up shop so we know how best to attack. Figured we would drive past today before we go back. Then we gather the troops, see who's playing for our side, and determine the best way to shut down Humphries's illegal surgery and capture him."

"What's to stop someone else from picking up where he left off?" Arabella asked.

The same thing had occurred to Owen as well. "That's always the challenge. We didn't know to look for the resurrectionists sooner, so they got a head start. Now, we'll be able to watch for the signs and shut them off quicker. This job is always like swatting roaches. Kill one, ten more pop up. I guess it's job security." He gave a lopsided smile.

"You might be right," Arabella agreed in a rueful tone. "In the meantime, I'll do some more digging and let you know what I come up with."

They thanked Arabella and took their leave, heading back to the carriage, but didn't speak until they were inside the vehicle's wardings.

"I take it you wish to get a look at Humphries's operatory?" Winston asked before he climbed into the driver's seat.

"Seems to be the next step," Owen replied. "Since I suspect we're going to end up there sooner rather than later."

"Very well. I'll scan for magical traps and protections and do my best to keep us tightly shielded. You might want to stay alert for more ghosts than usual," Winston told Owen. "I have a suspicion that for all of Humphries's successes, he's probably also had a deadly learning curve."

The carriage left the stable and moved into the crowded Chicago streets, threading its way among delivery wagons and coaches. They quickly left the more prosperous areas and headed into a warehouse district that was much less traveled and looked hard used.

Most of the buildings bore faded signs, but there was no way to tell whether those enterprises were still active or merely marked where they used to do business. Owen guessed that most were empty and disused or had new squatters eager to avoid notice.

A few sheets of newspaper blew across the empty street. Compared to Chicago's vibrant downtown, it was hard to imagine this ghost town was part of the same city.

"Want to bet the cops don't make regular patrols in this area?" Owen looked out the carriage window, glad they weren't on foot despite their advantages with weapons and magic.

"Probably not. If the other businesses are legit, they sure don't look prosperous, or they aren't spending their money to impress the neighbors," Calvin agreed.

Their coach was warded, and they all had protective amulets. Winston sat in the driver's seat, and his witch senses and magic swept the area around them as discreetly as possible to avoid raising alarms.

Not many people were in sight. That wasn't surprising for an area that didn't cater to retail traffic, but it added to the aura of disuse and abandonment.

"I wonder how many other illegal enterprises are in the other buildings," Owen mused.

"Probably plenty. Which means people mind their business and aren't likely to report something odd to the police," Calvin agreed.

"No obvious security guards."

"If people could see them, they'd wonder what needs guarding. Kinda defeats the purpose of being inconspicuous," Calvin pointed out.

Owen opened his senses to the spirits. He could see them like a translucent overlay, hidden figures who remained connected to this place long after their deaths.

Young boys were probably cutpurses or pickpockets. The women look like streetwalkers. The older toughs might have been Mob, gang members, or common thieves. A couple of them look like they blundered into the wrong neighborhood and didn't make it home.

"I think I caught a glimpse of some guards loitering in a few doorways." Calvin kept his revolver on his lap, as did Owen, just in case. "I can't imagine what else they'd be doing here."

"Anyone doing business here probably needs plenty of guards," Owen replied. "I'll be interested to see what Winston picks up. My magic isn't nearly as powerful as his, and I can sense the wardings. There's a very strong sense of being unwelcome. I know Winston has spells on the horses, but I'm honestly surprised that the ambient magic isn't making them balk."

They didn't slow down, keeping an even speed as if they were hapless travelers who took a wrong turn.

The closer they got to Humphries's building, the more ghosts Owen glimpsed. *They look confused like they don't know how they got here. Mostly teens to thirties—makes sense for prime bodies. All male, which would go with replacing limbs for their enforcers.*

Owen's heart went out to the ghosts who looked so lost. *Bad enough that they were murdered, but they've found no rest on the other side.*

Back in his Army days, Owen had heard the belief that people who lost a limb couldn't move on to the afterlife without a complete body. That had always seemed ridiculous to him. Now, he hoped more than ever that wasn't true.

"There's a large black delivery carriage beside Humphries's building," Calvin noted. "Plenty of room for a body in there."

"The building has enough space for a big generator to create the electricity he needs," Owen observed. "And if the other buildings are largely deserted, there are fewer people to notice odd smells and lights."

They didn't linger, not wanting to call attention to themselves.

Owen breathed in relief when they returned to more trafficked areas and came into sight of their Pullman car.

"Go in and get warm," Winston told them when they got back to the train station. "I'll return the carriage and start on dinner."

They headed for the Pullman, but Owen came to a dead stop a few feet away and threw his arm out to stop Calvin. "Someone left us a present."

A severed hand lay on the platform in front of the Pullman's door.

"I guess Humphries figured out we weren't professors." Calvin wrinkled his nose in disgust.

"Or his witch saw through the spells," Owen remarked. The body part wasn't fresh, and despite the cool day, it stank.

"Do you think Arabella could make anything from it?" Calvin asked.

"I'm not traveling with that." Owen shivered and looked around at the thankfully empty section of platform. He found a metal trash can, which he used to scoop up the putrid hand. Owen carried the can to a different siding, stuffed newspapers on top of the contents, and dropped a lit match, sending it up in flames.

"Message received," he said when he returned to Calvin. "Question is—who sent it?"

Since it came without packaging, Calvin's touch magic couldn't offer clues.

Winston bustled in after they had gotten settled in the parlor, and they told him about the severed hand.

"What did you make of the warehouse?" Owen asked. "I did pick up on some ghosts, and I know there was strong magic in play, but I'm sure you could sense more than I did."

Winston nodded. "Very much so. The warehouse is heavily warded, with protection spells and distraction magic so people simply don't notice it. That takes some high-level witchery, so Humphries has skilled practitioners helping him. We'll need to consider that in any plan of attack."

"I was afraid of that," Calvin said. "What else did you sense?"

"I'm wondering how the electricity Humphries uses to awaken a body part vies with the magic that keeps the limb alive," Winston said. "I'm guessing that's where the technology witches come in, but there's an inherent conflict between the magic and electricity that poses a big challenge."

Owen went to check the telegraph tape that recorded any missed messages in Morse code on a long streamer of paper.

"Got a message from Louisa," he told Calvin. "Said she'll be by this evening."

"Good. I still feel like we're missing important pieces."

A sudden, blinding pain stabbed through Owen's head. He knew Calvin was calling his name, but all Owen could do was put his hands to his temples and slump to the floor.

The train car seemed to disappear, and in its place, Owen found himself back at the restaurant where they had met with Luca Conti. But instead of Conti, Owen only saw the black-clad *strega*, and recognized the woman as Maria Bianchi, the Conti-Bianchi Family matriarch—and top witch.

"A war is coming. No good can come of it. I do not want my family dragged down. I can keep them from joining the conflict. I will try to rally the covens of the other families, but I can't guarantee they will also abstain. Luca is doing what he can to dissuade the others." The old woman's raspy voice sounded as clearly in his mind as if she stood beside him.

"Why are you helping us?"

"What that man is doing is unholy. It defiles the dead and the living. Act soon. The longer this goes on, the more likely that other families will be persuaded to join in the abomination. I cannot hold the covens together for long."

With that, the vision ended. Owen found himself lying on the floor, gasping for breath, held in Calvin's arms.

"Owen? Thank God. Are you okay?" For all that Calvin was a seasoned agent, he sounded completely panicked.

Owen groaned. The vision left behind a splitting headache. Before he could say anything, Winston hurried in with a pot of tea and a mug.

"You're awake and alive. Good to see. When you can sit up, I brought tea—and willow bark."

"It was a vision," Owen managed. "Sent by Maria Bianchi. A warning—and an offer to help."

"You can tell us more once you drink the tea. Magic like that leaves a nasty headache," Winston said.

"Magic? Calvin echoed. "I thought the Pullman car was spelled against any outside powers."

"I hadn't anticipated a witch of that strength sending a vision. Since she's technically an ally, the warding may have permitted the intrusion. I assure you, I'll find a way to close that loophole as soon as I can," Winston replied.

Calvin helped Owen sit and held the teacup for him to drink. "Your hands are shaking too badly—you'll have it all over you."

Owen sipped the hot beverage, willing the jitters to stop. "Maria Bianchi had a business proposition." The others listened as he relayed what the *strega* had told him.

"That's an alliance I didn't anticipate, but I won't turn it down," Calvin replied when he ended his recap.

"I'm surprised but not shocked," Winston said. "The Mob *stregas* have to be strategic. Mafia is their business, and their families are like rival companies."

"We need to move quickly while she can hold the agreement together," Owen said. "If the Mob covens side against us, I don't know if we're strong enough, even with our allies, to stop Humphries and his witches."

Calvin helped Owen to a seat on the couch as Winston refilled his cup and returned a few minutes later with a tray of cookies.

"Eat. No one plans a war on an empty stomach," Winston told them.

Owen thanked him, and Calvin poured more tea. "Talk to me," Calvin said. "What are you thinking?"

"I feel like things are coming to a head, and we're a step behind," Owen admitted. "We're missing some information, and we're running out of time."

"Maybe more pieces will fall into place when we meet with Louisa tonight," Calvin said.

"I had better get a start on dinner then." Winston headed back to the kitchen.

"Feeling better?" Calvin asked as Owen finished his second cup.

"Less disoriented. Her vision packed a punch. That's a scary-powerful witch."

"Who, at least for the moment, is on our side. I'll count that as a win," Calvin pointed out.

They settled in with the day's newspapers, scanning for any information that might mean more than it seemed on the surface. Soon, the aromas from the kitchen made Owen's stomach growl.

Winston called them to the table and served a perfectly braised chicken, along with fingerling potatoes, green beans, and cookies for dessert.

"Excellent, as always," Calvin said, and Winston beamed.

"How did we get so lucky? He can shoot, hex, and cook," Owen teased.

"An army moves on its stomach, and so do secret agents," Winston replied, clearly pleased at the praise.

At seven, a knock came at the door, and Winston brought Louisa to meet with them in the parlor.

"Coffee?" he asked.

She looked frazzled and relieved. "Yes, please. Hot and strong. It's been quite a day."

They took their seats, and Louisa removed her hat. "First, tell me what you've found out."

Calvin and Owen took turns catching her up on their latest findings. Louisa listened intently and nodded as they spoke. Winston brought coffee and a plate of cookies.

"All of that tracks with what I'm learning," she said when they finished.

"What's your news?" Owen refilled his cup.

"I've found the money trail. Arnold Miller, the big meat packer entrepreneur, is funding Humphries," Louisa told them.

"Meat packer? God. If I think too much about that, I'll be sick," Owen said.

"You know, that makes sense. A guy like that is used to slaughterhouses. Not much probably turns his stomach. He's up to his hips in pig pieces all day long," Calvin ventured.

"If I throw up, I'm aiming at you," Owen warned.

Calvin grinned. "No, you won't. Winston would make you clean it up and probably hex you for sullying the carpet."

"I'm still digging, looking for direct ties between Miller and Humphries. Want to bet he either owns the building you saw tonight or rents it?" Louisa went on.

"Sounds logical." Calvin agreed. "He might have owned the slaughterhouse where we think Humphries's necromancer sicced the dead cows on us." Calvin and Owen took turns providing a shortened version of the attack to catch her up on the action.

"Back to the meat packer," Owen said. "Slaughterhouses use a lot of saws and knives. People probably lose fingers and hands fairly often. Being able to put them back together would benefit the company."

Calvin frowned. "Sounds like expensive treatment for low-paid workers."

"If Humphries can reuse parts from dead bodies, there's an ongoing supply," Owen answered. "And think of the loyalty. Loyal workers don't go on strike."

After the deadly Homestead Strike in Pittsburgh several years before, the idea of protesting workers walking off the job struck terror in the hearts of factory owners.

"If the people Humphries fixes are bespelled by him in some way, that also makes them much less likely—or able—to protest," Louisa pointed out. "The other good news is that we've got support from some nearby Pinkerton agents and Pearl's gang. So don't start any fights without us."

"That should be interesting." Calvin chuckled. "Pinkertons and outlaws on the same side."

"We also have Arabella's coven—and maybe some of their friends,"

Owen said. "And now we know Maria Bianchi and her coven won't take Humphries's side, and neither will the other Mob covens—for now. Not a bad coalition. If the other Mob families stay out of it, we could have a chance."

"The families all have strongmen and *stregas*. There could definitely be advantages for a crime syndicate to being able to fix their injured guards," Calvin pointed out. "And bosses won't all share the same ethical qualms Maria Bianchi has."

"There's talk of friction between the Conti-Bianchi family and the Russo-Lombardi family," Louisa said. "The Contis have a strong hold, but the Russo-Lombardis are aggressive. The law enforcement folks I've talked with would prefer to see the Contis stay at the top of the heap. They're killers, but not psychopaths." She winced. "Or at least, not as bad."

"I get it," Owen said. "The enemy of my enemy is my friend. If the Contis can be reasoned with and aren't out to burn down the city, it's better than other alternatives."

Owen knew working with the Mob was part of life in Chicago. Organized crime was so deeply embedded in everyday affairs that eliminating it would probably take more force than even the US Army could muster. The Mob gained loyalty from the neighborhoods it controlled through beneficence programs for the residents, helping with food, rent, and medical expenses. Each Mob family protected their own turf, and in return, the residents didn't side with the cops.

Since the City of Chicago had yet to offer comparable help to shift loyalties, Owen didn't imagine that scenario would change anytime soon.

"Does it follow that the Russo-Lombardis are supportive of Humphries?" Calvin asked.

"I'm trying to find out, but that's my working theory," Louisa said. "And the other families have closer ties with one side or the other, so they're sitting it out until someone throws down the gauntlet."

"Which side is stronger?" Owen set his cup aside.

"Before Humphries entered the equation, the Contis," Louisa said.

"But with Humphries and his replacement parts and his witch, that could change."

Calvin swore under his breath. "Are you saying the balance of power in Chicago's underworld hangs on this case? How come we never get the easy ones?"

Louisa smiled and patted him on the arm. "Because the home office knows you're just that good." She finished her tea and stood. "I need to be off, but I didn't want to wait to share the news. I'll be in touch."

Winston walked her to her coach, where her bodyguard/driver waited, and Owen heard the hoofbeats fade as they drove away.

"No pressure, huh?" Calvin joked with grim humor.

"None at all."

Winston came back in and dusted his hands. "Well, that was informative. Nothing like raising the stakes to make it interesting."

Owen gave him a dour look. "Interesting isn't the word I would have picked."

After Louisa left, Calvin and Owen spent an hour working crossword puzzles from the day's newspapers, passing the time in companionable silence, seated close enough for their knees to brush.

Late in the evening, Winston came into the parlor with an envelope. "A messenger just brought this for Owen." He handed off the letter.

Owen frowned when he saw the handwriting. "It's from Steven," he said, although there was no other name on the outside.

He opened the sealed envelope and made sure to hold the pages so Calvin could see. Owen harbored no romantic feelings for his old flame but knew that Calvin held a twinge of understandable jealousy.

"We've had more close calls, and I'm sure there's a saboteur among us," Owen read out loud. "I've been spending more time in the stables to observe and overhear the workers talk. If I'm in a stall, they often don't realize I'm there.

"There's a guy, Jed Smith, who always seems to be close enough to see what's going on whenever something happens," Owen continued. "I can't prove he's behind the accidents, but you were always the one who told me to trust my intuition. He's got the night off, and I'm going to follow him. It might be nothing, but come by tomorrow morning, and I'll fill you in. I promise to be careful. Steven."

"Dammit!" Owen muttered, nearly crumpling the letter in frustration. "I told him not to play detective on his own."

"Whatever he was going to do, he's already doing it," Calvin said. "You're too late to stop him, and there's no telling when he'll get back. Cross your fingers and go see him tomorrow. I'm sure he'll take precautions."

"Goddamn cowboy," Owen swore. He knew Calvin understood that worry lay behind his anger. Steven had proven to still be a friend, and for the sake of their shared past, Owen wished him well and wanted him to be safe.

Did he feel he still needed to prove something to me after all this time? I don't want him to put himself in danger to impress me.

"How about if I read today's installment of the adventure story in *The Times* aloud for us?" Calvin suggested as Winston left the room, only to return minutes later with a tray that held a bottle of whiskey and two glasses. "Take your mind off things before we go to bed. Then you can go first thing in the morning while Winston checks back with Arabella, and I stop at the library."

Owen couldn't fault Calvin's logic, although he couldn't silence his worry. He appreciated his partner's efforts to distract him, but even the gripping serialized story didn't completely hold his attention. If Calvin noticed, he didn't comment.

That night, they lay close together in bed, content to hold each other. Owen's mood was off, and sex was far from his mind. Calvin seemed to read him as well as he usually did and kept him close.

"I want to wrap up this case and get out of Chicago," Owen confided. "I haven't had another vision or a ghostly warning, but my intuition is telling me to be more careful than usual."

"We are being cautious," Calvin said. "And once we solve the problem, we can leave the city behind. I'm hoping our next case is somewhere a little less complicated."

Owen rested his head on Calvin's shoulder, taking comfort in the warmth of his body and the faint trace of his aftershave. "I'm okay as long as we're together, no matter where they send us."

Calvin pressed a kiss to his temple. "Absolutely. Now try to get some rest. Love you."

"Love you too," Owen murmured, holding on tight.

"BE CAREFUL." Calvin kissed Owen goodbye.

"I always am," Calvin replied with a jaunty salute. "You can fill me in on Steven's news over lunch."

Owen's stomach still felt unsettled. He had toast and tea for breakfast, something Winston hadn't overlooked. Owen assured Winston that his stomach was only mildly upset. The look Winston gave him suggested that their witchy valet suspected more lay behind his reaction, but he didn't press the issue.

When Owen arrived at the Wild West show fairgrounds, he saw several police carriages. Concerned there had been another incident, Owen strode up to the gate and brandished his badge.

"What's the problem, officer?"

The cop read his ID and grimaced when he realized a fed was intruding. "Got another murder. This place has the worst luck."

"What happened?"

"Why does the Secret Service care?"

Owen bristled. "Government business. Fill me in."

Before the cop could answer, Owen heard a familiar voice.

"Oh, thank God you're here. I didn't know how to contact you." Harry, his escort from Owen's first visit, ran up, ignoring the cop. Harry's eyes were red, and he was clearly distraught.

"What's going on? Where's Steven?" Owen suddenly feared the worst.

"Steven's dead." Harry looked like he might burst into tears.

"Dead?" Owen reeled, taking a half-step backward. "What happened?"

When Harry wasn't able to answer, Owen turned the full fury of a federal agent on the cop. "Officer. I want details, or I'll be in your boss's office to yank your badge. Now, dammit."

Anger glinted in the cop's eyes at being outranked, but he kept his temper. "The victim was found outside the main gates this morning, but the body had been dead several hours by then. Bled to death."

"Gunshot? Stab wound?" Owen slipped into the cold efficiency of his role to temper his reaction, although he wanted to join Harry in weeping.

"Not exactly. The body was missing a hand and a foot. They weren't found with the body, and he clearly bled out somewhere else," the cop reported with the dispassionate tone of someone who hadn't known the person, hadn't been their friend and one-time lover.

Owen's stomach lurched. "Was there anything with the body? A note of some kind from the murderer?"

The cop shook his head. "No. You were expecting something?"

"Sometimes crazy people make a statement," Owen replied as his mind spun. Steven had tracked someone he thought might lead them to Humphries. Clearly, Humphries had found him—and taken vengeance.

"Not this time. Any other questions? I've got a mess to clean up," the cop snapped.

Owen shook his head, and the cop strode off.

Harry returned. "It's terrible," he sobbed. "Who would want to kill Steven? He was a good guy."

"Yeah, he was," Owen said quietly. "Is anyone else missing? Steven mentioned a guy named Jed."

"It's still early. Not everyone works mornings," Harry replied. "Jed's one of the locals. I haven't seen him today. You think someone here killed Steven?"

Owen weighed his answer. He didn't want to put Harry in jeopardy by knowing too much, but he burned with the desire to avenge Steven's death. Right now, fury carried him forward. Later, there would be time for grief.

"Not exactly," Owen hedged. "But if any employees suddenly stop coming to work, it's suspicious. They might have seen or heard something."

"I'll let the boss know if that happens," Harry said. "Why would anyone do such a horrible thing?"

"Because some people are sick," Owen muttered, as close to the truth as he could manage. "Will the show make arrangements for burial?"

"I don't know," Harry said. "The police took the body. No telling when we'll hear back. And we're not from Chicago…Steven was from out West, but I don't think he had family."

"Broken Bow, Oklahoma." Owen pulled the place from memory. He felt numb. "No family." He handed Harry his card. "If the show won't cover his burial, contact me, and I will."

Owen felt a sudden lurch as a vision overtook him. He felt surprise, then terror, and then nothing and knew Calvin was in trouble. His panic intensified when he couldn't re-establish the usually constant vague awareness of his partner that Owen had come to take for granted.

"Are you okay?" Harry asked.

"No. I've got to go." Owen ran back to his hired coach, ignoring the cop's judgmental glare.

"Main public library," he told the driver. "Fast as you can—someone's life is in danger."

Please be safe, Calvin. I never should have let you go alone. But Owen knew that as protective of each other as he and Calvin were, their jobs as government agents meant they couldn't go everywhere together. Owen had trusted in Winston's amulets for protection, but he feared that the madman who had killed Steven might have found a way around the magic.

"Wait for me," Owen snapped at the driver, jumping out when the wheels had barely stopped turning. He hurried up to the front desk and managed a strained smile for the librarian.

"I'm looking for a man who would have come to view some of the special collections earlier this morning." Owen gave Calvin's description. "Have you seen him?"

She nodded. "Yes, but you've just missed him, I'm afraid. He wasn't feeling well, and a couple of men helped him to a coach about half an hour ago. I'm sorry."

Once again, Owen searched but his psychic connection failed to find Calvin. *Please don't be dead. Please, please don't be dead.*

Fury mingled with fear, and the need for vengeance kept Owen on his feet.

Humphries has Calvin.

Chapter 9
Calvin

Calvin woke slowly with a pounding head, tied to a chair in a warehouse. While there were a lot of storage buildings in Chicago, Calvin bet that this was the location Owen, Winston, and he had ridden past not long ago.

Bins, crates, and shipping containers lined the walls, stacked atop each other. The space felt vast and cold, but most of it lay shrouded in shadows. A few overheads and work lights illuminated the immediate area around Calvin, and he was glad he hadn't come around in the pitch dark.

This has to be Humphries's lab. Shit. How did I get here?

He remembered going to the library, a quick errand while Owen took care of other business. Calvin had gone back to the stacks to find a book. He sensed someone nearby and reached for his gun, knowing he was in trouble, but then felt a needle slide into his skin, and everything went dark.

How long have I been out? Do Owen and Winston know I'm missing yet?

A chill went through him. *Am I a hostage—or a sacrifice?*

"You're awake. Good. I was beginning to think they gave you too large a dose. What would be the fun in that?" Dr. Jeremiah Humphries looked up from where he stood over an operating table, gowned and masked for surgery.

A man lay strapped to the table, and a severed hand sat on a small cart next to Humphries.

"You've been so interested in my work—I thought you should see it in action before you make a contribution," Humphries continued.

Contribution. He's going to kill me and take the parts he needs. I could be dead and harvested before Owen knows anything's gone wrong.

"You should be grateful—very few people get a front-row seat to my work. It's proprietary, after all," Humphries went on, seemingly unperturbed by Calvin's lack of response. "In fact, I think you may have even known the donor in this case. That annoying security chief from the Wild West show. He couldn't take a hint to back off."

Steven? Oh, God. That's going to wreck Owen.

And when he finds out I've been taken? I might not get rescued, but I'll definitely be avenged. He won't leave anything standing.

Shit. I thought we'd have more time together. Calvin's fear and anger turned to sorrow.

"I have a process for selecting donors," Humphries continued. "There needs to be a general compatibility in body size and type, skin tone, age, and gender. The part needs to be fresh, so the death should be recent—the more so, the better."

The man on the table was still breathing, naked except for a sheet.

"When I first started, I scavenged the only bodies I could get— from vagrants and drifters. They usually weren't in the best health, and that made the operations riskier than usual," Humphries monologued. "But I made do. Most went well. There were some complications, but that's how science advances."

Calvin wondered how many of the early patients survived and decided he didn't want to know.

"I refined the process," Humphries continued. "But the real breakthrough came from matching donors to recipients. No longer depending on chance or making do with the best available. Once I started selecting a good fit, the results improved."

Calvin held his tongue. There was no point in antagonizing

Humphries when Calvin had no means of escape and no certainty of rescue.

I might find out everything we wanted to know and not be able to tell Owen. I'll have died in vain.

"You're just the right fit for my next patient," Humphries said. "Close to the same height and build, similar musculature and coloring. There will always be a scar, of course, but on wrists and ankles, that's easy to hide. It won't be an exact match, but you'd be surprised how few people are truly observant."

"Ever considering going legitimate—and soliciting voluntary contributions from the families of accident victims or the healthy dead?" Calvin asked. As uncomfortable as the idea of patching a living body back together with pieces from corpses made him, the real crimes lay in murder and in violating the bodies without consent.

"The authorities and the Church have played merry hell with doctors transplanting thyroids," Humphries said as he worked to reattach the hand on his sleeping patient. "I can't imagine them supporting a more visible replacement. Even if the family agreed—which would be surprising—the process to get approval would take years. Decades. And in the meantime, people who need help do without."

Yeah, you're a real philanthropist, Calvin thought. Humphries was no doubt well paid for his efforts and risks, and without approval from the authorities, rich mobsters and criminals were the beneficiaries because they could afford his price and weren't concerned about the ethics.

"Why Steven—the guy from the Wild West show?" Calvin tested the ropes binding him and found them too tight to slip, so he knew his best bet was to keep Humphries talking to buy time.

"He was in excellent health, a good match for age and build," the resurrectionist said. "And the fact that he was acquainted with you and your partner sealed the deal. I don't allow people to get in my way."

Calvin looked around; his training kicked in, even though he probably wouldn't survive to report his observations. Humphries had set up one part of the huge, empty space with lights and equipment for a mobile surgical unit, similar to what the military used. Most of the old warehouse was dark and unused, cluttered with boxes and stacks of wood except for supply bins of materials for Humphries's work.

Since Calvin didn't see any indication of living quarters, he guessed the doctor had found somewhere else for lodging.

The building had electricity, which was still uncommon. That powered the lights, but even more importantly, it fed the big metal box that Calvin guessed was the special electrical generator Humphries used to revivify his monstrosities.

A huge knot of wires ran from a spot in the outer wall into the machine and more straggled from the front of the equipment, where Calvin supposed Humphries connected his patient to bring the limb back to life.

His captors had peeled off Calvin's gloves. When his skin touched the chair or rope, images of past prisoners…sacrifices…flashed in his mind, and he felt glimmers of their pain and fear. He knew he had to push through the horror if he was going to have any chance of saving himself.

"The surgery itself is tedious." Humphries seemed unable to avoid playing to an audience, even a captive one. "There's magic involved, and electricity, but if the part isn't reconnected well, it won't get blood, and the person won't be able to feel it. Magic helps with that and preservation, but it's much more than just sewing the skin together and hoping for the best."

He wants to be hailed as a medical genius and be famous and accepted. I bet it galls him to have to hide in a warehouse and serve criminals instead of rich patients.

"How long do they last? The parts you stitch on?" Calvin couldn't help being curious.

"That depends," Humphries replied. "My earlier efforts were a learning curve, and I refined my technique. Having good source materials makes a big difference."

Source materials. Stolen parts from people's bodies.

"It also depends on the age and health of the recipient as well as that of the donor," he went on. "But if all the aspects are positive, the attachment can last for quite some time. The oldest ones still functioning are over a year old. I don't know yet what the outer limit is."

The donor dies and the limb is only good for a year, maybe a little more. The recipient could have lived reasonably well as an amputee without requiring a murder. Seems like a bad bargain.

"I can guess what you're thinking—too high a price for too short a time," Humphries guessed his unspoken judgment. "The people who get another year or more of having a working hand or foot don't think so. This world isn't kind to people who can't do for themselves."

"When the limb fails, what then?" His agent training couldn't pass up the chance to learn more, even though he suspected Humphries's willingness to brag came from his certainty that Calvin wouldn't leave alive.

"I'm working on that," Humphries said. "The trick is to remove the new part before it goes septic and infection kills the recipient. But as the reattachment process and the magic supporting it become more sophisticated, I'm confident we can overcome that issue. Maybe even have a part last for the rest of the recipient's lifespan."

Technically, if the new part goes bad and kills the person, it did last for the rest of the recipient's lifespan. The span is just shorter than advertised.

"What's in it for your witch?" Calvin ignored the throbbing pain in his head. He hated being drugged, although he allowed that it was probably better than being hit over the head.

"All the usual things," Humphries replied. "Money. Notoriety. Access to rich, grateful patrons. Bragging rights. It's certainly not something that just any witch could do."

"You've got a tame necromancer?"

"Hardly. Avery is a colleague, an equal partner. He's a visionary who sees how magic and medicine can work together." Humphries's passionate tone was a shift from his earlier clinical coolness. "Right now, medicine and magic stand divided by prejudice on both sides. Can you imagine the possibilities if that barrier was broken down? Accredited doctors who are also skilled witches, practicing their full abilities in the open, without fear of being persecuted."

Because witch doctors have such a good reputation.

"Being the pet of the Conti Family isn't big enough for you?" Calvin figured he had little to lose by keeping Humphries talking since it forestalled his death and gave Owen the ghost of a chance to come to his rescue.

Humphries laughed. "Luca Conti doesn't have the balls to be my patron. That hag who runs his coven has all kinds of Catholic compunctions about bringing what was dead back to life. Rich, isn't it, considering Easter?"

"So who? Someone looking to knock the Contis down a peg? The Russo-Lombardi faction?" he guessed, remembering the conversation with Louisa the previous night.

"The world is changing, and people who can't change with it will be left behind." Humphries had continued to stitch his patient as he talked. The man remained unconscious, but Calvin saw his chest continue to rise and fall. "The Russos aren't afraid to seize an advantage and use it to their favor. They'll be the top of the Chicago Mob, and I'll make sure their soldiers are nearly unkillable."

Nice fantasy and probably made a great pitch to your patron. Delivering on it could be a real bitch.

Calvin shifted on his chair. His bonds didn't give him much leeway, but the slight movement was enough to let him know that the thin saw blade hidden in the waistband of his pants was still there. He thought he could work it loose with his fingers. He just needed time to cut through the ropes to free himself before Humphries made him the next project.

I'll give escaping my best shot, but the odds are slim. And if Humphries's witch shows up, I'm out of luck.

I wonder if Owen has realized yet that I've been taken? And if he does, will he rush in half-cocked to rescue me and play into Humphries's plans?

They had come so far, learning to trust and letting down long-held barriers. Both of them had old scars that healed slowly, damage from the past, but they had brought out the best in each other. Their relationship was still new, but their bond was already surprisingly intense.

Owen will blame himself for my death and Steven's. It's not his fault, but he'll never believe that. Will he quit the service? Can Winston stay with him, or will he be reassigned?

Calvin thought back to leaving the train car that morning, glad they had kissed and traded endearments. *At least Owen knows I love him, and I hope he knows I'd never leave him if I had a choice. We haven't had nearly enough time together, but I've tried to tell him how much he means to me. I wanted a lifetime. It doesn't look like we're going to get that. I'm sorry, Owen.*

If we got lucky, we could have eventually retired together or done something less risky. Other agents manage. We can't marry, but we could make our own vows, pledge the rest of our lives together.

Looks like the rest of my life is going to be far too short.

Calvin swallowed hard, steeling his nerves and keeping his face impassive, determined not to show any weakness or fear. He wouldn't give Humphries that win, even though inside he felt cold with terror.

How does he intend to kill me? Probably depends on what parts he wants to take. I imagine a bullet to the head would be too kind. To the heart? Or maybe slitting my throat? Does it matter how much blood I lose before he cuts off whatever pieces he wants?

The thought of Owen finding him like that, not just dead but mutilated, filled Calvin with remorse. *I shouldn't have gone to the library without backup, knowing what was going on. Should have waited for Winston or Owen.*

I took precautions. Humphries just got the drop on me. And now Owen pays a price as well.

Calvin didn't doubt that his death would bring out a darker side of Owen that he had glimpsed, an obsessive determination that would stop at nothing to achieve its objective. Reined in, that ability made Owen a brilliant agent. But bent on revenge, Owen was likely to break rules, cross lines, and sacrifice himself to atone for Calvin's death.

Killing me is likely to destroy both of us. I wouldn't be any better if the roles were reversed.

Humphries had stopped talking, intent on finishing his work. Calvin maneuvered so that his fingers could reach the spot in his waistband that hid the saw blade. Escaping was a long shot, but Calvin intended to go down fighting.

"You get to see the best part." Humphries sounded excited as he pushed his patient's gurney toward the large metal box.

"Where's your witch? Shouldn't he be here?" Calvin couldn't help being curious. He worked at the saw blade and then twitched his fingers to begin the slow job of fraying his ropes.

"The magic was done before you woke up. Don't worry—he'll be back when it's time to preserve your parts. Hands and feet bring a premium," Humphries gloated. Calvin repressed a shudder.

"Here's where science changes the world." Humphries attached wires linking the big box to the patient's newly sewn-on hand.

"Behold!" He threw a lever, and the box lit up, whirring and beeping as it came to life. Electricity crackled around nodes at the top like a deadly halo. Calvin could feel a charge in the air, even at a distance, like the air before a thunderstorm.

The whole contraption whined, and then the man's hand began to twitch and jump, coming off the gurney and several inches into the air. The patient, until now drugged senseless, opened his eyes and screamed, and his body arched against the restraints.

Calvin sawed faster. The blade slipped, and blood slicked his fingers. He tightened his grip and ignored the pain.

I don't have to cut through all of the ropes. Just enough to wiggle free.

There are plenty of knives on the table. Any of them should do nicely. The witch isn't here, and Humphries is only human.

I might not succeed but attacking beats waiting to be killed.

The smell of ozone and burnt flesh filled the workshop, and Calvin fought the urge to gag. The patient, eyes wide and chest heaving, gripped the gurney white-knuckled with his original hand. He looked pale and terrified, but the fingers of the new hand twitched, and Humphries clapped with exultation.

"Another success!" Humphries celebrated.

Calvin felt the rope give, and he struggled with all his might. One loop snapped, and the rest fell to the ground. He launched himself out of his chair, ignoring the pounding in his head, and dove at Humphries.

Humphries recoiled, bumping the gurney and sending it rolling. It hit a crack in the cement floor and toppled, which snapped the restraints and dumped the patient onto the floor. The man lay still and did not try to crawl away.

Gunfire sounded outside the warehouse, barely audible above the whine of the generator. He hadn't seen any guards, and now Calvin guessed they had been watching the street to avoid interruptions.

Owen. He's come to rescue me—and I sure hope he's got backup. I've just got to play for time.

Calvin grabbed a scalpel from the cart, tamping down his gift to ignore the graphic images the item raised in his mind. He brandished it at Humphries, who stared at him wide-eyed as if he couldn't grasp how suddenly his advantage had disappeared.

Humphries ran at Calvin with a knife, and Calvin dodged, slashing his stolen scalpel across the doctor's face. Humphries screamed and staggered. Calvin shoved him with the implement cart and sent him flying back against the machine. Humphries threw his arms wide with the impact and snagged his lab coat on the generator's big lever.

The massive generator threw up a shower of flame and sparks. Humphries, caught on the lever, shuddered and twisted like the side of beef in the galvanism exhibition as the voltage surged through his body. Fire shot from the machine, setting Humphries alight and catching in the trash that lay piled against the walls. Humphries screamed as the flames rose, engulfing him and burning him alive.

The piles of trash and stacked wooden boxes caught quickly. Billowing smoke filled the warehouse with a choking haze that burned in Calvin's lungs.

"Calvin! Calvin!" Owen's voice came from the direction of the doorway.

"Over here!" Calvin dropped to his hands and knees to keep his head below the smoke. He crawled toward the fallen patient, fearing the worst.

He rolled the man over, and the arm with the stitched-on hand flopped to the side. Calvin checked for breath and heartbeat but found neither.

"Calvin!" Owen fell to his knees beside him. "Thank God. You're alive."

"We've got to get out of here before the smoke gets worse," Calvin replied. "Humphries and his patient are dead." He pointed toward the charred corpse that still hung from the generator, which was now engulfed in flames

Owen pulled him to his feet and grabbed him by the arm. They hunched low, running toward the door. Whatever was in the heaps of wood and paper burned fast, creating a thick, stinking cloud that made them cough and stung their eyes.

Owen led the way, throwing the door open and hauling Calvin outside.

They heaved for breath, sucking in the cold air and wiping away tears.

"Owen! Calvin!" Arabella hurried to meet them. "Is Humphries dead?"

"Yes. That was his headquarters," Calvin told her. "He's got a necromancer helping him."

"He *had* one, you mean," she replied with a smug smile. "We trapped him when he left the warehouse. Maria Bianchi wrung out a confession before she killed him. He won't be helping anyone take over Humphries's role, and after today, I doubt any other ambitious witches will be looking to take the job if someone is stupid enough to try to take Humphries's place. Get out of here. I'll make sure the whole place burns to the ground." Arabella waved her hand.

Calvin glimpsed Louisa and several men he assumed were Pinkertons holding a periphery around the warehouse. The gunfire hadn't come closer, but it sounded like a pitched battle was underway just a few blocks away.

"Pearl and her gang are keeping the Russo guards busy," Owen told him. "We're going to try to go around them and keep our heads down. Don't get shot."

When they rounded the corner, shots pinged in the brick wall near them. Owen dragged Calvin into a doorway.

"You got him?" Pearl shouted over her shoulder as she reloaded, barely pausing before shooting again. She glanced from Owen to Calvin. "Get out of here. We'll handle the goons."

They were barely another street away when an explosion shook the ground, and they turned to see a fireball where the warehouse had been. Calvin felt certain that Arabella would ensure that nothing remained of Humphries's equipment or his work.

"Winston took a contingent of witches to Humphries's house," Owen told him. "He'll make sure that no papers or files survive."

"How did you find me?" Calvin couldn't stave off another coughing fit. Owen rubbed his back.

"I'll tell you everything later," Owen promised. The wail of sirens sounded, growing louder. "Let's get out of here. I don't want to explain any of this to the cops."

By the time the fire engines and police wagons thundered past them, the gunfire had ended. Calvin knew that the witches would have vanished into the shadows and that the Pinkertons as well as the mobsters and Pearl's gang would be long gone.

A carriage rolled up beside them, and the driver lowered her hood so they could recognize Louisa. "Get in."

They climbed aboard, and she snapped the reins, setting them off at a brisk pace. Two men Calvin didn't recognize were already inside.

"Pinkertons," Owen said. "Louisa's people." He turned to the two agents. "Thanks for the assist."

The younger of the two men grinned. "There's never a dull moment. Glad we could be of help. Whoever hired the warehouse guards did a lousy job. They folded as soon as we showed up in force."

"Probably weren't getting hazard pay worth the risk," Owen said. "Better than fighting tooth and nail to the last man."

The younger Pinkerton looked at Calvin. "You the guy who got kidnapped? Your partner called out everything except the cavalry to rescue you."

"Thank you," Calvin said. The smoke had made his throat sore and roughened his voice. "Did any of your people get hurt?"

"Nah. The guards didn't have the belly for a real fight," the older detective replied. "We trussed them up and left them for the cops. I don't imagine they're upstanding citizens."

Once the dust settled, Calvin figured they would hear Pearl's side of the fight with the Russos, either from Louisa or Pearl herself. He wondered how Maria Bianchi's standoff with the other covens had gone and whether tonight would tip the balance of the Mob wars between the Conti family and the Russos, but at the moment, he was too exhausted to care.

Squashed into the carriage, Calvin's knee bumped Owen's, providing needed comfort. There were so many questions he wanted to ask, but not until they were safe in the Pullman car, in the privacy of Winston's wardings.

After we shower. I can still smell the smoke and charred flesh. I hope we've got menthol rub.

"I'll be in touch," Louisa called to them when she stopped the carriage at the train station.

"Thanks for the lift," Owen replied.

"Thanks for a fun night," she said with a jaunty mock salute.

The carriage waited until they were inside the Pullman car before it drew away. Winston hurried to greet them.

"Oh, thank the gods. You're alive." He appraised them for injuries.

"Have any luck at Humphries's apartment?" Owen asked Winston as he guided Calvin out of the foyer and toward the bathroom.

"The wardings were easily broken, and apparently he never thought anyone would search for his notes and materials," Winston said with a sniff of judgment. "We sent all his papers up in flames, took the things we couldn't burn so we could destroy them in a safe place, and did a powerful cleansing ritual."

"He won't be going back," Owen said. "Calvin killed him."

"Serves him right." Winston's tone was pure steel.

Now that the crisis was over and he wasn't dead, Calvin felt the adrenaline fade as the events of the day hit hard. "Shower—and tea."

"The water is already boiling. I'll have tea ready in a trice," Winston replied.

"I bet Calvin's got a roaring headache too, between the knock-out drug and the smoke," Owen told Winston.

"I have just the thing for it," Winston replied. "Clean up. I put fresh clothing for both of you in your rooms already. I'll have something to eat fixed by the time you're done."

Calvin let Owen steer him to the bathroom and strip off his clothes, which were stained with smoke and blood.

"I'll burn them," Owen promised as he added his soiled clothing to the pile. "Let's get you clean."

Calvin allowed Owen to maneuver him, glad not to have to think. He figured that shock was finally setting in, considering his close call. His head no longer throbbed, but Calvin feared it might come back at full strength if he moved wrong.

Owen pressed up against him, skin to skin. The hot water sprayed over them, and Calvin felt his shoulders relax just a bit.

"Let me get your face first." Owen's voice, calm and careful, sounded like he was talking to a spooked animal. He wet a cloth and gently wiped it over Calvin's forehead, then down over his eyes and cheeks, washing away the sweat and grit.

"Better?"

Calvin nodded. Now that he was safe, he felt close to tears and didn't want to break down.

"Shh. It's okay, whatever you need," Owen said in a voice just above a whisper. "Cry, rant, scream. I'm here."

"You came for me." Calvin could barely hear his words above the water.

"Of course I did. Hell itself couldn't stop me."

Calvin's breath hitched. Owen pressed a kiss to his neck. Then he soaped up his hands and began to lather Calvin's shoulders and chest, working his way down his arms and noting where the rope had abraded and the hidden saw had cut his fingers.

"I'll take care of those when we dry off. Let me make sure they're clean."

Owen washed Calvin's back and buttocks, then down both legs before rising to clean his groin, gentle but not sexual. Grateful as

Calvin was to be home safely with his lover, sex was the furthest thing from his mind right now.

"Time for everything later," Owen murmured as if guessing his thoughts. "We can have glad-you're-alive sex in the morning. No rush."

There were so many questions Calvin wanted to ask, but the hot water and clean scent of soap drove them all from his mind. His body responded to Owen's care, working its own version of touch magic.

Owen took his time washing Calvin's hair, massaging his scalp before rinsing under the water. "There. Just like new," he said with a strained smile. Calvin could see the toll the day had taken in Owen's eyes and knew they needed to talk about Steven, although he couldn't muster the courage just yet.

Owen shut off the water and reached for a towel, gently drying Calvin first. He patiently held out Calvin's clothing and helped him dress, then hurried into his fresh outfit.

"You should eat."

"Not hungry."

Owen looked at him fondly. "I know. But you need to heal and that takes energy. I'm sure Winston has something that you can stomach, even if it's just tea and crackers."

Calvin knew Owen was right, although his stomach balked at the thought of food after everything he had seen.

Winston had left a pot of tea, two cups, and a plate of crackers with sliced cheese in the parlor, guessing correctly that sitting at the dining table seemed too much right now. A glass of water and some willow bark sat next to the food.

"Stay close." Calvin reached for Owen's hand.

"Oh, I swore I'm never letting you out of my sight again." Owen's tone told Calvin that he was only partly joking. Then again, it was the second instance in their short time working together that Calvin had been kidnapped, so he figured Owen came by his opinion honestly.

I wouldn't want Owen to be the one in danger, but I don't want to make a habit of getting nabbed.

Owen joined him in nibbling the light refreshments, and Calvin figured that his partner was equally shaken and grief-stricken.

"I shouldn't have let you go alone." Owen broke the silence. "I know, we're secret agents, and the library isn't usually high risk, but look what happened."

"It should have been safe."

"But it wasn't. I almost lost you," Owen replied in a choked voice.

"I didn't see anything dodgy when I got to the library." Calvin's voice sounded numb even to his own ears. "I went back to the stacks for a reference book, and that's when they got me. Some sort of injection. I don't remember anything after that until I woke up in the warehouse tied to a chair."

"When I got to the library, they said you had felt unwell, and your friends helped you to a carriage," Owen picked up the story. "I knew then Humphries had you. I am so, so sorry."

"You know…about Steven?" Calvin murmured.

Owen caught his breath and blinked a couple of times before he nodded. "Yes. By the time I got there, the police were already on site. I heard the details from Harry, one of the helpers at the show. When they said he was missing a hand and a foot—" Owen choked on the words and shook his head. "That's when I knew it was Humphries. And if he killed Steven, he'd come after us."

"I'm so sorry."

Owen bowed his head, and when he looked up, he had regained control. "Steven was a companion at a time when I was very alone. We were never in love, but he was kind and got me through a tough patch. I'll always be grateful. He was trying to do the right thing, following up on a lead. He didn't deserve what happened to him."

"I know."

"And then, when you went missing, I sort of lost my mind," Owen confessed. "Winston and Arabella stopped me from charging in, but it was a near thing. I was so afraid that by the time we rallied the troops and attacked, it would be too late, and you'd be…gone."

"I'm glad you came when you did. It was a close call. Too close. If I hadn't managed to cut the rope—"

"But you did," Owen said stubbornly. "You got loose and killed Humphries, even after everything."

"Killing him was accidental," Calvin admitted. "Lucky break."

Owen shook his head. "You saw a chance and took it. Takes a damn good agent to do that after being drugged." He frowned. "How's your head? Those drugs are awful stuff."

"Getting better," Calvin replied. "The willow bark will help."

Once the food was gone, Calvin leaned against Owen, who wrapped his arms around him tightly. He knew Owen was trying to be strong for him despite his own fear and grief.

They sat in silence for a while. Calvin was content to listen to Owen's breathing and feel his heartbeat. Owen kept running a hand up and down Calvin's upper arm as if to assure himself that Calvin was solid and real.

"All I could think was that you and I hadn't had enough time," Calvin finally said without looking up. "We'd only just found each other. I couldn't stand the thought of leaving you. I know…we haven't talked about the future a lot…but in my mind, I saw us growing old together, as close to married as folks like us can be. Forever."

He blushed at the admission. "Maybe it's silly—"

"Not at all," Owen jumped in. "I've thought about it too. Just wasn't sure what you wanted."

"You. I want you," Calvin said, stubbornly defiant. "Come hell or high water."

"Then I'm yours." Owen pressed a kiss to Calvin's temple. "Forever."

Calvin took his hand, threading their fingers together. "Forever."

We should get a bonus for stopping a Mob war as well as solving the Humphries case," Owen said as he dug into the quiche Winston had made for them, celebrating their safe return. Two days had passed since the fight at the warehouse, long enough for Calvin to physically recover and for Owen to make sure that the loose ends were resolved.

"What did you hear?" Calvin paused with his fork on the way to his mouth.

"The Russo-Lombardi alliance didn't survive the finger-pointing when details started to come out about Humphries," Owen told him.

"Maria Bianchi and her allied covens had a nasty showdown with the Russo-Lombardi witches," Arabella spoke up. She and Louisa had joined them for a farewell brunch before they left Chicago. "I didn't press for details, but some problem witches have gone missing, just like Humphries's necromancer."

"Imagine that," Calvin murmured. "What have the papers said about the warehouse fire?"

"The articles said that an electrical fault burned the warehouse and several nearby vacant buildings." Owen paused to sip his coffee. "They blamed an apartment fire the same night on an oil lamp that tipped over."

"Hmm. That's…plausible." Calvin reached for another slice of toast.

"I told headquarters that we closed the case. They were miffed that we didn't hand over Humphries's notes for safekeeping, but I told them everything was lost in the fire." Louisa smirked.

"Like anything good could have come out of letting those exist," Calvin muttered.

"My thoughts exactly," Owen replied. "Winston made sure Humphries's notebooks didn't survive."

"As for the Russo-Lombardi-Conti war, the papers ignored it like they usually manage to overlook Mob activity." Louisa set aside her muffin. "But there was a small article about the murder of the Wild West show's security director."

Calvin looked up, and Owen knew his partner could see the sadness he felt over Steven's death. "What did it say?"

"Only that Steven had been brutally murdered by an unknown assailant. They left out details of the mutilation, probably to avoid a panic," Louisa said.

"Just as well, since we took care of the problem," Owen added with a bitter note in his tone. "The show is leaving town early. I can't imagine how they could stay after everything that happened."

"No, they couldn't," Calvin agreed quietly. He reached to take Owen's hand and squeezed. "I'm so sorry."

"Yeah." Owen let out a long breath. "So am I. But there's no changing it."

Winston came in, bearing a steaming pot of coffee to refill their cups.

"Along with stopping Humphries, all the revelations and activity has led to some reshuffling in the witch world," Arabella added. "Thanks to the necromancer's death and the coup Maria Bianchi's coven pulled off against the rival witches, the covens tipped the power to more responsible practitioners," she reported.

"And the Contis are firmly ensconced as Chicago's top Mob family, which, considering the alternatives, is the best we could ask for," Louisa added.

"Is it always this exciting when you two come to town?" Arabella teased.

"We're the life of the party," Owen replied.

"Never a dull moment when we're around," Calvin chimed in.

"We couldn't have done it without you both, and all your friends," Calvin said. "What about Pearl?"

"Got a telegram letting me know she'd gone West after leaving Chicago without problems and reminding me of our deal," Louisa said. "I pulled a few strings to get lesser charges dismissed. As long as she plays nice with us and lends a hand if we need it, the remaining charges could languish for a long time and eventually go away as well."

"And the toughs her gang and your folks were fighting?" Owen asked with a glance at Louisa.

"The cops took the suspects that my Pinkertons left trussed up for them, and as it turned out, they had plenty of prior arrests," Louisa replied in a droll tone.

"I'm shocked."

"Figured you would be," she snickered. "My team gets credit for a high-profile bust and having a hand in averting a Mob war. Pearl gets bragging rights and her charges put on hold. She and her gang took the midnight train out of Chicago that same night before the police could catch wind of them."

"Do you think anyone will try to pick up where Humphries left off?" Calvin looked away and fiddled with his napkin. Owen felt certain that his partner still had a long way to go to recover from the horrors of his abduction. "After all, there was supposed to be a rift between the traditional witches and the technology mages. I wouldn't think the technology fans would give up on science so easily."

"My Pinkerton team paid a visit to Augustus Gordon, the showman doing the galvanism demonstrations," Louisa replied. "We were…persuasive. He packed up and left town, closing the show permanently. If someone tries to fill Humphries's shoes, I don't think it will be Gordon—even if he has the talent, which I don't think he does."

"And my coven will make sure that the other covens find out what *really* happened to Humphries and his necromancer," Arabella added. "Short of nailing his head to a door, that's a pretty severe warning, even by Chicago standards."

"Someone on the Russo side was backing Humphries," Calvin put in. "What's to keep them from throwing money at someone to try again?"

"First and foremost, Maria Bianchi and her coven," Arabella pointed out. "That is one scary powerful lady—not counting the magic. With the Russos at odds with the Lombardis and their witches defeated, they're going to be busy defending their turf, let alone trying to raise the dead."

"And the ambitious up-and-comer from the Russo side that put the alliance together and tried to take on the Contis was found dead in his sleep—presumed heart attack," Louisa reported in a dry tone. "The boss on the Lombardi side that he was working with has vanished— no one seems to know whether he skipped town or took a deep dive into Lake Michigan."

"My money is on the lake," Owen said. "Tied to a cement block."

"That will shake things up." Calvin sat back in his chair. "It should reshuffle the balance of power and the pecking order with the Mob families for a while. Keep them so busy watching their backs they won't have time to play with dark magic."

"We can hope," Owen muttered. "As for the wealthy slaughter-house owner, the society page said he and his family have gone on an extended European vacation and may consider selling their Chicago plant."

"Do tell," Calvin replied with a chuckle. He looked to Louisa. "More of your doing?"

She shook her head. "I thought about it, but he was gone before we got to him. Maybe he just saw what happened to Humphries and decided to get the hell out of town," Louisa said. "Doesn't look like he has the balls to try again. But if he does—Arabella and I will find him."

Once breakfast was over, Arabella and Louisa took their leave, promising to keep them posted about any related developments.

Calvin yawned and stretched. Owen looked at him with concern. "How are you feeling?"

That morning, Calvin had awakened in a panic, glassy-eyed and terrified, fighting for his life against the sheets that had gotten tangled around him. He had nearly punched Owen in the face as Owen tried to restrain him to soothe his fears.

A word from Winston had put Calvin out like a drug, and with Winston's help, Calvin shook off the nightmare before waking the second time. Calvin had been contrite and embarrassed, but Owen wasn't surprised at the reaction, given what happened—and how bad it might have been.

"Do we have a new case yet?" Calvin asked. Owen guessed his partner wanted to prove he was fully recovered, although only two days had passed since the big fight.

Owen shook his head. "No. I told them we were due some time off. Winston is arranging to connect us to a train headed up to Elkhart Lake, a resort town where we should be able to catch our breath."

"Honestly, I'm—"

"Don't say fine." Owen glowered at Calvin. "You're not fine. No one would be *fine* after what you went through, and frankly, we're all worn out. A few days won't make a difference. There will still be plenty of criminals left to catch."

Calvin's cheeks reddened. "I don't want the brass to think I'm not fit for duty."

Owen suspected that Calvin was embarrassed about his night terror and reached for his hand. "You damn near rescued yourself, got out of the ropes, and killed the mad doctor. I'll fight anyone who says that isn't good enough."

Calvin's grateful smile told Owen his partner read the resolution in Owen's eyes. "Thank you. But it really was a team effort."

Owen sighed. "Yes, for the big picture. But we came to Chicago to stop Humphries, and you did it. That counts for a lot. The rest of us mopped up the other pieces."

By noon, the train attached to their Pullman steamed north toward Elkhart Lake. They arrived mid-afternoon, and Winston shooed them from the car so he could provision and set up for their stay.

The quaint, well-kept town seemed sleepy compared to Chicago's constant bustle. Other than a couple of resort hotels and restaurants, the town catered to summer visitors who came for golf and boating.

Calvin and Owen walked side by side, admiring the cottages and remarking on the change of pace.

"Not bad for a vacation, but I'd go nuts if we were here for long," Calvin said. "Besides, I'm terrible at golf."

Owen laughed. "I think the quiet is part of the charm. People come to take the cure of fresh air away from the pressure of the city. Stare at the water. Go fishing. Read a book."

"It sounds rather romantic when you put it that way." Calvin bumped shoulders.

"It could be." Owen had given Calvin space since his rescue for them both to deal with the situation and its aftermath. He hungered for Calvin's touch, but they needed to keep their distance in public.

They found a bench near the lake and sat to watch the birds and boats. The air held a chill despite the sunny day and blue sky.

"Thank you." Calvin nudged Owen's knee with his own. "For suggesting this. For stopping me from rushing into the next case. For taking care of me. You knew what I needed better than I did."

Owen smiled fondly. "Give Winston credit for finding the location. He was my co-conspirator."

"I'm trying to let go of what happened. But it comes back in my dreams. I'm pretty sure I've got battle fatigue," Calvin admitted. "Sometimes I'll be doing something else and see an image from the lab or catch a whiff of something, and I'm right back there. I don't know how to make it stop."

Hidden by their coats, Owen took his hand. "It'll get better with time. Maybe not right away, but after a while. It might never go away completely, but the flashes will get fewer and farther between. At least, that's the way things have been for me." Owen had his own nightmares and traumatic memories from near-misses and cases gone wrong.

"Winston said that Arabella knows witches who can help if it gets too bad. They don't take away memories, but they use magic to help people handle them better," Calvin replied. "I hope I don't need it, but it's nice to know there's an option if I do."

Winston had already given Calvin a powder and worked light spells to help him sleep more soundly.

"When you have a bad spot, talk to me," Owen urged. "I will always listen."

"I know. Thank you."

After a while, they headed back to the Pullman, walking in sync, as always. Inside, the smell of dinner made Owen's stomach growl.

"Perfect timing. The food will be ready soon. Steak, baked potatoes, and a salad," Winston said. "A well-deserved feast."

As they ate, the conversation stayed light. Winston had made inquiries at the station about local things to see and do, and he shared ideas of how Calvin and Owen could explore the area.

"How are you planning to spend the time?" Owen was pleased to have ideas to keep Calvin busy and give him something good to think about.

"I intend to visit the nearby museums and the library. I'm intrigued by the local history," Winston replied. "And when I'm not otherwise needed, I have a novel I'm eager to finish reading."

After dinner, Winston brought a bottle of good brandy into the parlor before leaving them to play cards. Calvin seemed distracted and jumpy, and his mind was clearly not on the game.

"How about we go to bed early?" Owen set his cards aside. "Let me make you feel better."

Calvin's quick agreement told Owen his partner was on the same page. Owen took Calvin's hand and led him to his room, closing the door behind them. He pressed Calvin against the wall, stepping into his space and kissing him slowly and deeply. Owen's fingers traced Calvin's cheek and neck, and his hands moved from shoulders to arms to hips, confirming that Calvin was solid and safe and *here*.

"Is this okay?" Owen asked.

"Yes, please. God, Owen, I need you to touch me. Make me feel good. Make me feel *you*."

Owen answered with another kiss, slipping his tongue into Calvin's mouth and nipping at his lower lip. He slid his hands up Calvin's chest to work the buttons of his shirt, then his own.

"Come on." He tugged Calvin toward the bed, then stopped beside it to divest them of the last of their clothing. Owen pulled Calvin down with him and took him in his arms, kissing him slow and deep.

"Top or bottom?" he asked barely above a whisper.

"Suck me," Calvin said. "And I'll do you. That's what would feel good right now. We can do more in the morning, but for tonight, that's what I want."

In response, Owen kissed Calvin on the lips and then slid down the bed, licking his way down Calvin's chest and belly. He swirled his tongue over the head of Calvin's already-hard cock, tasting his pre-come, pleased that Calvin was already hard and leaking for release.

Owen took Calvin's prick in his mouth as far as he could, all at once. Calvin gasped and arched, and Owen let his tongue trace his partner's sensitive skin as he wrapped his hand around the base, setting up a rhythm. With his other hand, he reached between Calvin's legs to fondle his balls and tease at his taint and hole.

"Not going to last long if you keep doing that," Calvin told him breathlessly, moving his legs apart to give Owen access.

Owen settled between his thighs, keeping up the rhythm with his hand as he licked and sucked. Calvin grabbed fistfuls of the sheets and moaned his pleasure, fighting the urge to cry out as Owen brought him to the edge and backed off more than once.

Owen felt his climax building and knew he wouldn't last for a second round.

"Need it," Calvin begged. "Make me come."

Owen redoubled his efforts, and it didn't take long before Calvin's come filled his mouth. Owen swallowed it all, continuing until Calvin gently pushed at his forehead.

"Too sensitive," Calvin said. Owen pulled off with a pop and a kiss. "God, that was so good. Give me a minute, and I'll return the favor."

"Already finished," Owen admitted. "We can steal the sheets from your bed."

"I'm sorry—"

"Don't be." Owen crawled up to lie beside him and took Calvin in his arms, holding him tight. "We needed to get that out of our systems. Proof of life sex. We can go slow next time. Neither of us was going to last."

"I know we've got a list of things to do," Owen said. "But I'm also fine with spending the morning in bed. I've got plans of my own."

Calvin looked up at him with a soft, fucked-out smile. "Count me in. Forever."

Afterword

Language has changed a lot since the 1890s. Words like "heterosexual" hadn't come into use yet, and "gay" just meant happy. There wasn't a polite term for being gay, and the word "homosexual" had just been coined in 1869 and carried a stigma. The least offensive terms were "nancy" or "molly"—Victorian slang for effeminate men or those who liked other men. The sting of those terms has eased over time by falling out of use and becoming archaic. I did my best to choose the least offensive terms that were also period-authentic.

Calvin and Owen recognize the danger that being different poses, but they accept themselves as they are, with little guilt or internalized negative views. As agents, they live outside of societal norms, and both have come to see their orientation as nobody else's business.

Where Calvin or Owen thinks about their "preference" for men, I do not mean to suggest that being gay is a preference. "Sexual orientation" is a contemporary term that would not have been used in 1897, so Calvin or Owen would think of the kind of person they felt drawn to—"preferred"—as a partner. This is also why they frequently think in terms of "men like me." That phrasing enabled me to make the point without requiring labels.

My goal with the choice of language was to minimize negativity

Afterword

and avoid modern hurtful terms while using words Calvin and Owen might have chosen. Given that being gay was illegal at the time, the repression and need to hide is historically accurate, just as it is also accurate that many people remained true to themselves and found companionship and love despite society's prejudice.

Ida Turnbull was a real person, a pioneering female reporter of that era who broke blockbuster stories and investigated powerful people. Whenever possible, I love to weave in elements from history. Sometimes truth is stranger than fiction.

You will see more of Calvin, Owen, and Winston, so stay tuned!

Acknowledgments

Thank you so much to my editor, Cassie Hess-Dean, to my husband and writing partner, Larry N. Martin for all his behind-the-scenes hard work, to my beta readers, and to my wonderful cover artist Deranged Doctor Design. Thanks also to the Shadow Alliance and the Worlds of Morgan Brice reader street teams for their support and encouragement, plus my promotional crew and the ever-growing legion of ARC readers who help spread the word!

I couldn't do it without you! And of course, thanks and love to my "convention gang" of fellow authors for making road trips and virtual cons fun.

About the Author

Morgan Brice is the romance pen name of bestselling author Gail Z. Martin. Morgan writes urban fantasy male/male paranormal romance, with plenty of action, adventure, and supernatural thrills to go with the happily ever after.

Gail writes epic fantasy and urban fantasy, and together with co-author hubby Larry N. Martin, steampunk and comedic horror, all of which have less romance and more explosions.

On the rare occasions Morgan isn't writing, she's either reading, cooking, or spoiling two very pampered dogs.

Watch for additional new series from Morgan Brice and more books in the Witchbane, Badlands, Treasure Trail, Kings of the Mountain, Sharps & Springfield, and Fox Hollow universes coming soon!

Where to find me, and how to stay in touch

Join my Worlds of Morgan Brice Facebook Group and get in on all the behind-the-scenes fun! My free reader group is the first to see cover reveals, learn tidbits about works-in-progress, have fun with exclusive contests and giveaways, find out about in-person get-togethers, and more! It's also where I find my beta readers, ARC readers, and launch team! Come join the party! https://www.Facebook.com/groups/WorldsOfMorganBrice

Find me on the web at https://morganbrice.com. You can also find me on Pinterest (for Morgan and Gail): pinterest.com/Gzmartin, on Instagram as MorganBriceAuthor, on YouTube at https://www.youtube.com/c/GailZMartinAuthor/ on Bookbub https://www.book

bub.com/authors/morgan-brice, on TikTok @MorganBriceAuthor and now on Bluesky as @MorganBrice.

Check out the ongoing, online convention ConTinual www.facebook.com/groups/ConTinual

Support Indie Authors

When you support independent authors, you help influence what kind of books you'll see and what types of stories will be available because the authors themselves decide what to write, not a big publishing conglomerate. Independent authors are local creators supporting their families with the books they produce. Thank you for supporting independent authors and small press fiction!

Don't miss where the action begins!

Peacemaker

Secret agents, forbidden love, danger, and magic!

Supernatural Secret Service agents Owen Sharps and Calvin Springfield meet on the train to their new assignment in St. Louis, and sparks fly between them. But it's 1897, and they need to be very careful—falling in love can be dangerous for men like them.

It's their first case together, investigating mysterious disappearances—including the two agents who preceded them. Grim evidence leads them to look for a darker purpose. Old ghosts haunt the railroad line, zombie rise, signs point to ritual sacrifice, and they suspect someone is trying to open the gates of hell.

Can Calvin and Owen stop the mayhem, thwart the vampires, and find true love, or will everything go up in smoke?

Peacemaker is a high-stakes steampunk MM romance thrill ride filled with found family, paranormal Pinkertons, intrepid reporters, myste-

Also by Morgan Brice

Badlands Series

Badlands

Restless Nights, a Badlands Short Story

Lucky Town, a Badlands Novella

The Rising

Cover Me, a Badlands Short Story

Loose Ends

Night, a Badlands Short Story

Leap of Faith, A Badlands/Witchbane Novella

No Surrender

Point Blank

Memory and Malice, a Badlands Novella

Shine Tonight, a Badlands Short Story

Thunder Road

Fox Hollow Zodiac Series

Huntsman

Again

Silent Partner

Fox Hollow Universe

Romp

Nutty for You

Imaginary Lover

Haven

Gruff

Trash and Treasure

A Taste of Danger: Subparheroes

Kings of the Mountain series

Kings of the Mountain

The Christmas Spirit, a Kings of the Mountain Short Story

Sins of the Fathers

Kings of the Mountain Universe

Roustabout : Carnival of Mysteries

Sharps & Springfield Series

Peacemaker

Equalizer

Treasure Trail Series

Treasure Trail

Blink

Last Resort

Secrets and Ciphers, a Treasure Trail Novella

Treasure Trail Universe

Light My Way Home, a Treasure Trail Novella

Witchbane Series

Witchbane

Burn, a Witchbane Novella

Dark Rivers

Flame and Ash

Unholy

The Devil You Know

The Christmas Crunch, a Witchbane Short Story

Sandwiched, Witchbane Short Story

Ambushed, A Witchbane Novella

Midnight on the Midway: Carnival of Mysteries

Castle Magic: A Caynham Castle Collection